I0733876

Black Erotica

Erotic, Adult Short Stories Written by Black Women featuring Older-Younger, BDSM, First Times, Anal Sex, Groups, Cuckold, Gangbangs, MFM, Lesbian, and Paranormal Fantasies

Jade St. James

© Copyright GO Publishing 2023 - All rights reserved.

The content contained within this book may not be reproduced, duplicated or transmitted without direct written permission from the author or the publisher.

Under no circumstances will any blame or legal responsibility be held against the publisher, or author, for any damages, reparation, or monetary loss due to the information contained within this book. Either directly or indirectly. You are responsible for your own choices, actions, and results.

Legal Notice:

This book is copyright protected. This book is only for personal use. You cannot amend, distribute, sell, use, quote or paraphrase any part, or the content within this book, without the consent of the author or publisher.

Disclaimer Notice:

Please note the information contained within this document is for educational and entertainment purposes only. All effort has been executed to present accurate, up-to-date, and reliable, complete information. No warranties of any kind are declared or implied. Readers acknowledge that the author is not engaging in the rendering of legal, financial, medical or professional advice. The content within this book has been derived from various sources. Please consult a licensed professional before attempting any techniques outlined in this book.

By reading this document, the reader agrees that under no circumstances is the author responsible for any losses, direct or indirect, which are incurred as a result of the use of the information contained within this document, including, but not limited to, — errors, omissions, or inaccuracies.

Contents

Introduction

I don't know if you've noticed, but it's hard to find erotic books and audiobooks by black women for black women. I decided to fix that!

My name is Jade. I'm a writer, editor, and teacher out of Brooklyn, NY. My specialty... erotica.

I talked with several of my writer friends and gave them this assignment: Write the stories you want to read!

And my queens delivered!

In this book, you'll find a wide range of these that turn us on. Everything from romance to the roughest hardcore scenes. Something for everyone.

I can't tell you how much fun I've had working on this project, and I know you'll enjoy it as much as I do.

Sit back, relax, and enjoy Black Erotica.

Climactic
By Kiara Keets

IMANI WALKED into Jenkins Creative Agency and happily greeted everyone she passed as she walked in the direction of Phillip's office.

Phillip Jenkins was her creative writing professor at the college over the summer, and he'd been the point of contact for her internship at Jenkins Creative Agency. An agency his parents—natural-born story-tellers in the theatre world—had created 30 years ago for all the writers in their local area that wanted careers in writing.

She knew he was her professor and mentor, but he was so fine!

During her internship, she'd worked with Professor Jenkins closely as he taught her the elements of great storytelling.

Every story has a beginning, middle, and end.

Every story has a setting, exposition, rising action, climax, and resolution.

During the internship, she'd met some of his colleagues who had written books that had garnered them a livable salary.

The two smiled at each other before Phillip greeted her by saying, "Good morning." He was seated at his desk, his white Polo shirt covering his broad shoulders and slender frame well. His mocha skin was free of blemishes, and his hair was a low cut with waves. She could get seasick looking at them.

Imani tried her best not to admire how plump his lips were, but as he asked, "How are you today?" All she could think about was how much better her day would be if he used them to kiss all over her body.

"I'm doing well," she said. "And you?"

"Everything is perfect!" His voice wasn't a booming baritone, but the voice of a smooth alto. "I can't believe it is your last day interning with us. You've been a joy. Have a seat."

Phillip was keeping his comments to himself, but he loved having her around. She had beauty and brains.

She smiled as she walked to the seat that had her facing him and said, "It's been a pleasure working with you and your team. You all have taught me valuable information to take my career to the next level."

Phillip smiled at her. He was pleased that this young woman had been listening and learning.

"We all here know you will be a great writer. If a position opens where we know your skillset will benefit us, we'll contact you for employment."

"It would be an honor to work for a company like yours. Thanks for keeping me in mind."

"My pleasure," he said. "Did you bring your final assignment?"

Phillip couldn't help but notice her radiant smile.

"You know I did. I finished it last week and printed it yesterday," she said. "Your administrative assistant has been holding it for me. I'll grab it now."

Her figure was concealed in a hot pink dress that came to her knees.

Imani gracefully got up from her seat, fixed her dress, and waltzed to retrieve the printed manuscript from his assistant.

Phillip was glad no one could notice that he watched her hips sway as she walked. He even looked at her perfect apple-shaped bottom that fit her frame perfectly. Her hot pink dress worked with her copper skin so well.

He sucked in a quick breath of air to calm himself down. In his 10 years of teaching, he'd never been romantically interested in a student. However, he'd developed feelings for her over the last few weeks. Feelings he'd never had in the classroom, but the quality time with this intern was different.

While taking her seat, she passed him her manuscript and told him everything on the rubric was in it.

"Remarkable," he said as he thumbed through it. "This is wonderful. How old are you?"

Imani scrunched up her eyebrows in suspicion. "I'm 21. Why do you ask?"

"I'm 37 and I wrote my first book at the age of 23. My parents already had this company, but I was too afraid to give them my book. I didn't think it was good enough. Finally, when I was 25, I had the balls to show them what I wrote. I published my first book at 26. Whatever edits I have for this, I'll send back to you. You might be able to publish it next year."

"Thanks for the encouragement, Mr. Phillip," she said as she looked into his eyes.

Imani was always in awe of him because of his beauty, but his worth ethic was impeccable. She also took a mental note that he was 16 years her senior. He didn't look a day over 30.

"I want to give you something I wrote, and I want some constructive criticism," she told him.

Phillip looked puzzled. "Wait. You had the time to write some more? Even though you have a part-time job, this internship, and that manuscript you just submitted?"

In a matter-of-fact tone, she said yes.

He was in awe. She really did enjoy writing.

"But this is a short story, and I want you to read it in your downtime."

She opened up the email on her phone and sent him the short story.

"I just emailed it to you," she said. "I hope you like it.

Phillip checked his emails on the desktop computer. Like clockwork, Imani's email was on top, and he saw the attachment for her story.

What he didn't know was that she had written an erotic short where he was the leading man and she was the leading woman who had mind-blowing sex. She hoped he liked it.

"If I have any notes for you," he said, "I have your number to contact you."

"Sounds good," Imani said. "Enjoy the rest of your summer."

* * *

As the day went on, Imani said her goodbyes to everyone at the agency, and before she knew it, it was time to get to her job. She hopped in her car to go.

Time was going by fast at work, and before she knew it, it was time for her 15-minute break. She looked down at her phone and noticed a text message.

When she opened it, she was surprised to see a text from her professor.

Imani. I started reading your manuscript for your final assignment and your characters are magnetic. But the short story you sent me – I have notes. Come to my place tomorrow and have a drink with me to discuss this further.

She was glad no one could see her blush, and she gave a shy smile before pondering how to respond.

Hey Phillip. Thank you for working so expeditiously. What time tomorrow?

Phillip responded that he was free the next day from 3 p.m. to 7 p.m.

She responded with:

That's a great window of time. I'll be there tomorrow at 4 p.m.

He told her he'd see her then and gave her his address.

Imani squealed with excitement. When she clocked off from work, she went home to figure out how to plan for her evening of notes with Phillip.

* * *

It was 3:55 p.m., and Phillip pulled fresh cheeses out of his fridge, grapes, crackers, pretzels, hummus, and wine.

He hoped she liked red wine.

He placed the snacks on a clean cutting board and grabbed a clean knife to slice the cheese.

Hearing a knock, he rinsed his hands off at the sink, dried them, and opened the door for Imani.

She was standing outside with her heart beating fast and her palms sweating. She was a mature young woman, but she wanted him to notice. She was so nervous, but she didn't want it to show.

He couldn't help but smile as he greeted her. The summer sun sparkled on her skin as he told her to come in.

The young woman walked in with a purse, a small notebook, and a pen. Her hair usually was in flat twists or corn rows, but this evening, a few strands of curls framed her face, and the rest was in a curly puff on her head. She was wearing a white T-strap shirt and pink skort. Her pedicured feet were in sandals.

"I'm glad you could make it," he said, leading her into the kitchen.

"Thank you for inviting me," she said, admiring his home.

When she walked in, a light, minty smell greeted her. His kitchen and den were beautiful, eclectic almost. While there were a lot of items from American folklore and art, she noticed trinkets of fantasy items. She noticed comic pieces and orishas.

"Everything looks good in here."

"Thank you," he said. "It took many years to get to this point."

She followed him into the kitchen, noticing that the green and white tracksuit set he wore complimented his frame.

"I was about to cut up these appetizers for us," he said pointing to everything.

"Would you like some help?" she asked.

He told her he would greatly appreciate her help.

For the next few minutes, they had small talk.

"I'm glad you're able to help me with my story."

"Ah yes," he said as he finished working with the cheese and started spreading out the crackers. "You didn't tell me your short story was erotic."

He stopped what he was doing to see her reaction. She gave a coy smile and said, "As an author, I shouldn't have. I just want to make sure the story evokes emotion."

"Oh, it evoked emotion," he said, opening the hummus. "I had to take a cold shower afterward."

Imani's jaw dropped at how open he was.

He moved the knife and cutting board out his way and leaned across the island to talk to her.

"Where did you get this idea from?" he asked.

"I had you and me in mind," she said. "Is that a problem?"

"Hell naw," he confidently said, letting his eyes wash over her face.

The two couldn't unlock each other's eyes, but Phillip did pour them glasses of wine.

"This ain't nothing but the exposition, Mr. Phillip," she said as he handed her a glass.

"How long until we get to the climax?" he asked her before winking.

She twisted her smile and looked at the ground then back at him.

"We didn't even get to the rising action, Professor," she said.

"Enough talking in riddles," he said. "Grab the drinks, and I'll place the charcuterie board on the tiny table."

They placed everything on the glass table and got comfortable on his loveseat.

"Your characters in the erotic are beautiful. I liked how you wrote the classroom as their sex room. Your imagery was on point, your words evoked emotion. She seduced him at her desk, then his desk, and it took a bit of coaxing, but he finally gave in to her. There's something I would change, though."

Imani was trying not to get too entranced in his

looks while she listened to him. She grabbed her notebook and pen to do so.

"What would you change?" she asked, ready to take notes.

"I'd have them seduce each other. You also wrote the professor as a nervous, clueless, submissive man. I'd write him a bit more confident and dominant."

She started scribbling down what he said.

Then she felt his big hand grab her writing wrist and said, "Stop writing. I can show you better than I could tell you."

Her heart started beating faster, and her words were stuck in her throat and she struggled to inquire, "What?"

He got up, stood over her, and spoke again.

"You had her calling the shots, which is a beautiful thing. Not every man wants a submissive woman, but he was too damn scared."

He pushed the notebook and pen out of her reach and pulled her up, only to sit them back down to have her in his lap. His arm was loosely around her midsection.

She let out a quick gasp.

Imani was cradled in his arms, but she felt good in them. They dreamily looked at each other.

He looked down at her lips, his eyes fluttered closed, and she made sure to meet his lips halfway.

His lips were moist, soft as pillows, and it was a tender kiss she didn't want to stop. He didn't stop the kiss either.

He was taking her breath away, literally, so she placed one of her hands on his chest to push him back.

Philip knew that type of push was small but could mean to stop. He pulled away and looked her in her eyes and said, "Are you okay?"

She nodded her head yes to catch her breath.

Phillip could be dominant, but he was a big believer in *No means no.*

So he watched her every move when she stood up and unwrinkled her clothes but was happy when she crawled back on his lap, this time straddling him.

Her knees were on opposite sides of his body, and she took his lips into hers. Her ass was like a magnet; his hands were drawn to it. He cupped her ass cheeks in his hands as he strongly kissed her back. He used his lips to suck her bottom lip. He wasn't going to stop until they were swollen.

Imani was not going to protest, especially when she felt his dick throbbing against her thigh. It probably wanted to be released from those joggers, but she had other things on her mind.

His lips moved from her lips to the crook of her neck, and she could have melted when he licked, kissed, and sucked the lower portion.

"Fuck!" she exclaimed as his motions sent her nipples and pussy into a frenzy.

He smiled internally at how well she was reacting to him. He moved to the other side of her neck to assault that crook. She rocked herself against his bulge. He gripped her ass tighter to rock her on it a bit longer.

If the loveseat wasn't so small, he'd have taken her right there, but he needed room to fuck her until her soul left her body.

He carefully lifted them off the seat, and when they were fully up, she wrapped her legs around his waist before standing on her own.

Once she stood up, she lost her balance a bit, but he held her tighter to him.

"Should we be doing this?" she asked out loud.

"We'll only do it if you're okay with it," he told her.

"But you're my professor. I'm 21. You're 37. What if I'm not good enough?"

"You know what the song says: Age ain't nothing but a number. What you lack, I'll be more than glad to teach you."

Imani blushed, and he gave her a quick peck on the lips.

"Now tell me what you want to do," Phillip said.

"I want you to fuck me like this is for one night only," she told him.

"Say no more," he said, walking her to his sofa. He walked to a cute, tiny gold and red chest on his fireplace and retrieved something out of it.

When he was in front of her again, she noticed he'd grabbed condoms. He placed them on the arm of the sofa.

She was thankful he was being proactive because she wasn't. She just wanted his dick inside of her.

He watched as she took her shirt off, and he did the same. They both got rid of their pants, and he smiled as he looked her up and down. She looked great with clothes on, but even better in her matching pink lace bralette and panty set.

She licked her bottom lip as he stood there in boxer briefs. His six-pack looked like it was sculpted by God, and she knew exactly where his happy trail ended.

"Now the professor in your story seemed scared to get intimate with his student," he said.

He helped her lay on her back on the sofa and said, "He should have laid her on the desk like this."

He rolled her lace panties down her legs, threw them on the floor, and took his boxers off. His dick was still semi-hard, but his main focus was her.

Imani was pleased. It was a little shorter than she'd imagined, but it looked thick as hell, and she wanted it.

He climbed on top of her and kissed her with so much passion she felt like he loved her.

He loosened her bralette to suck on her nipples. Her body writhed underneath him as his lips sucked on the sensitive left nipple like a baby sucks on a bottle. The fingers of his free hand gently squeezed on the other nipple. She felt her juices flowing in her pussy.

It was making Phillip hard as hell hearing her moan.

His lips moved to her right nipple as his fingers squeezed and tugged the other.

Imani felt a shiver down her spine as his lips trailed down to her stomach, to her thighs, and she openly gave him access to her pussy.

He wasted no time snaking his tongue through the folds of her pussy lips. He did every pattern—zig-zags, a circle, the letter P—between her pussy lips.

She was so ready for him to put her dick inside of her pussy, but she could tell he was the type of man that liked to take his time. She held on to the sofa because she felt like she was about to squirt all over his face.

"Phillip, please," she managed to moan.

"Please what?" he asked as he pulled his tongue out of her.

"Please give me your dick."

Phillip didn't even eat her out the way he wanted to, but he listened to her. He grabbed a condom off the sofa's arm and used his teeth to open it. She smiled seeing her love juices over his chin.

He used the backside of his hand to wipe it off. He pulled the condom out and put it on himself.

Imani watched as he climbed back on her and closed her eyes when he kissed the lips on her face.

She tasted good on his lips.

Her mouth opened in a perfect "o" shape when she felt two of his curved fingers slide into her as he kissed her.

Her pussy was wetter than a Slip-N Slide, and the noises it made were reminiscent of a fresh bowl of macaroni and cheese.

Phillip held his dick in his free hand, stopped kissing her, and looked down at the beautiful pussy beneath him. He locked eyes with her as he rubbed the tip of his dick on her folds and clit.

Imani was starting to feel nervous under his gaze and covered her eyes with her hand. He removed her hand and said, "Naw. Let me look at your eyes while I'm fucking this pussy."

And just like that, he thrust his whole dick inside her. That action made an "Oh shit!" come from her lips.

It was hard to keep her eyes open and focus on him as he rhythmically thrust inside of her. When his eyes pulled away from hers, he reached over her to use the arm of the chair for leverage. His strokes were longer and quicker, and she made sure to tell him, "Don't stop."

"Fuck you feel so good, Imani," he grunted as he held the arm of the chair. He felt like he was swimming in her pussy and was about to drown.

"I'm coming," she said out loud.

He pulled off the arm of the chair and used the top cushion of the sofa for leverage to make sure he rocked in her until she hit her climax.

She clenched her pussy around him a few times to get herself to the finish line. He must have felt it because his moans sounded more animalistic.

Imani knew she couldn't stop now. She stopped clenching and made sure her thrusts matched his. Their rhythm was like no other. His strokes weren't too fast, slow, or hard, but just right. She couldn't believe she was about to come in a matter of minutes.

It had been a while since a man had made her come so fast. She was getting tired, but she was on the final strokes of her climax when she felt butterflies in her stomach and felt like she had to pee.

Before he knew it, Phillip watched as her body did slight quivers underneath him, and he made sure to not stop his strokes. He wanted her to ride out her climax, and she looked sexy as hell doing it.

Imani finally put her hand up on his chest to stop. He slowed down his strokes and pulled out.

They were both breathing hard, and she smiled as she thought about what had just happened.

He walked to the kitchen trash can to dispose of the condom. He washed his hands and approached her on the sofa. He sat next to her and pulled her into his arms.

Phillip peppered kisses from her ear down to her collarbone.

"And that's how you should have written the professor," he said in between kisses.

"I damn sure should have," said the young woman. "I didn't know it was going to be that fantastic. You fucked the student better than I wrote it."

He chuckled. "I noticed you didn't give them a second sex scene," he told her.

"It wasn't needed. But If you were to help me write another scene for them, how would you write it?"

"I can show you better than I can tell you."

Ghostly Benefits
By Kim LaRoux

"I don't know why you want to stay in this haunted ass house by yourself," Tonya told her little sister Aliyah.

"It's probably not haunted," Aliyah retorted. Even though she wasn't so sure herself.

The two were unboxing Aliyah's hair supplies in her new house. Their great-aunt Georgia had died two weeks ago and left it to her in her will.

Twenty-five-year-old Tonya had received $100,000, while twenty-three-year-old Aliyah received Georgia's house, which was worth the same amount.

Their Aunt Georgia was what folks back in the day called a spinster. She'd never married, nor did she have kids. Her brother, Abraham, was Aliyah and Tonya's grandad. She adored the two young women like they were her grandchildren.

"I don't care, sis," Tonya said to Aliyah. "Remember when we would hear weird noises in the house when we would spend the night?"

"T. It's an old house. It's going to make noises. Besides, Auntie Georgia never mentioned ghosts or spirits in the house."

"Whatever," Tonya said, carrying a few hair products in her arms and placing them under the sink in the bathroom.

Aliyah remembered the stories folks had told about her great-aunt's house. They always heard creaks, they would see the outline of a man in the window, and they said small items would be rearranged overnight.

She was hesitant, but she needed this house. She couldn't afford an apartment; she had just enough funds for utilities and food. She was about to start a new job at a call center. Her parents had helped her come up with a financial plan so she could maximize her financial stability. .

The two girls continued to unpack. They were so glad their male cousins had done all the hard work earlier. They'd knocked down cobwebs, swept, mopped, vacuumed, polished, and shined the house. Then they'd moved the boxes in for Aliyah.

For the next three hours, the two unboxed everything—her small set of dishes, her clothes, bedding, a new bed set for one of the guest bedrooms, and her awards over the years. She planned to keep the regal pieces of furniture and accessories her Aunt Georgia had had. She was going to keep as much of it as she could.

She told herself in a few years when she had enough money, she'd update the house again.

It was going on 4 p.m., and their dad came to bring them some dinner.

"Dad! You are amazing!" Aliyah said while making herself a plate.

Her dad was a fabulous cook. He'd made them pot roast and homemade biscuits.

When all three of them sat at the table, he told the girls he wanted Tonya to stay with Aliyah tonight.

"Daddy! No!" Tonya exclaimed. "You know I don't want to stay here."

"I don't trust this house. Stay with your sister," he told her.

The two kept going back and forth until Aliyah spoke up.

"I'm fine. If things get out of hand this week, I'll ask someone to spend the night with me. Now please, let's eat in peace."

It was 9 when her sister and dad left.

She was already spooked being in the house, but them giving her tips on how to survive through the night was nerve-wracking.

So she kept all the lights on while she prepared for her first night in. The young woman retreated to Aunt Georgia's room, which was now hers. She remembered spending a lot of time with her there.

Aliyah grabbed her night clothes and headed into the bathroom for a shower.

She put some music on—perfect for dreaming.

These were songs her aunt always played. First, it was "Try Me" by James Brown. Then music by Smokey Robinson and the Miracles. She even played the classic "Stay" from *Dirty Dancing*.

She was a little jumpy when she heard squeaks and creaking in the house. She cursed when she dropped her soap because of it.

Aliyah started to feel a little bit better, even though she did feel a presence in the bathroom with her. She sang the lyrics to "Stay" to get out of her head.

When she flossed and brushed her teeth, her favorite song played, "I Put A Spell on You" by Nina Simone. As she sat on her bed in a purple teddy, she put oil and lotion all over her body. She started from her shoulders and went to her arms, massaged the slippery lubricant on her breasts, and down her muffin top.

When the song ended, she let it replay. As Nina Simone's voice calmed the atmosphere in the house,

Aliyah yawned, crawled under the covers, and drifted to sleep.

The next morning, when she awoke, the sun's rays danced around in her room. She smiled to herself when she realized she'd made it through the first night unscathed. She walked into the bathroom to start her morning routine. She couldn't believe how well-rested she was.

She called Tonya and told her she'd made it through the night.

Tonya exclaimed, "Thank goodness."

Aliyah shook her head at her sister's dramatics.

She got dressed in a skirt and a tee. She rubbed on her onion booty as she looked in her full-length mirror. She had to admit, her ass looked fat.

The young woman walked to the two guest bedrooms in the house and admired the different things in the rooms. While looking at the old pictures, she noticed what people had said for years—she favored her aunt.

She smiled at the realization, but again she felt a presence in the air.

Aliyah exclaimed to the "presence," "I know ghosts aren't real! I'm sure I just feel my aunt's presence in this house and nothing more."

She smacked her forehead and said, "Liyah. You sound stupid. Calm down."

The young woman found two boxes she hadn't unpacked and began to finish the job.

Afterward, she called her "friend," Jason, to come over. She had met Jason at a party months ago, and she was still deciphering if she wanted a romantic relationship with him. Whatever they had going on, she loved him for his tongue.

His dick wasn't the best, but it always scratched her itch. He always ate her pussy like she was the finest plate of food.

She made herself a cup of hot tea while she waited for him.

When he came over, she gave him a tour of the house. He was enthralled with the place. He said he always heard stories about how haunted the house was.

Aliyah told him she'd made it through the night fine. He still told her to be careful.

She walked him to her bedroom and laid him on her bed. She opened the window to get some fresh air in. She unzipped his jeans and pulled his dick out. Jason was calling out her name while she gave him head on her bed. But she stopped when she heard him say, "Did you hear that?"

"Hear what?" she asked, looking up at him.

"Something closed?"

"That's your imagination," she said, putting her forehead on his abs to get back to work.

"Liyah. I'm serious," he said, pulling himself out of her mouth.

He looked around the room to see what would have closed.

"The window," he said. "What in the world?" He got off her bed to examine it.

Aliyah's heart started to beat fast. She felt like the wind wouldn't have closed the window.

This was day two in her house, and she didn't want to admit it, but it might have been a ghost.

To calm herself, she asked Jason if they could lie down for a while.

He obliged. He was the big spoon as they drifted to sleep.

When they woke up, Jason had to go back home. She didn't want him to. She wanted someone to stay with her. She felt like someone was in the house with her, and that window situation was weird.

While preparing for bed that night, she shouted to the house, "If you want to mess with me tonight, you can't. I love this house, and I refuse to be scared to live here."

The twenty-three-year-old climbed into bed and drifted to sleep.

She drifted into the dream world.

Her dream was set in the 1960s, an era in America she'd always admired. In the dream, she was dancing at a juke joint. All of the men wanted to dance with her.

While they were all handsome, there was one that wouldn't stop dancing with her. His hair was fried, died, and laid to the side. The side part in his hair was so sharp, she knew she'd cut herself touching it. His golden brown skin glistened with sweat with how hard they were dancing.

"Georgia. Let's dance the night away," he said in her ear.

"Aliyah," she corrected him.

"Georgia. I'm Barnabas. Don't you remember me?" he whispered in her ear.

She was going to correct him again, but Aliyah heard the phone ring.

Ring! Ring!

Aliyah groggily woke up. The dream was so good, she didn't want it to end.

Why was the mystery man calling her Georgia?

Her room phone continued to ring. It was her parents calling her. She answered the phone, had small talk, and prepared herself for the day.

That night before bed, Aliyah played all the 1960s songs she could think of. She wanted to feel like she was at a juke joint.

While playing the music in the kitchen, she swayed her hips and did the mashed potato to every song that played. She made herself a plate of food, and before she knew it, it was time for bed. She took a shower, oiled her body, and drifted to sleep.

She dreamt of Barnabas again.

This time they were at a pool. His chiseled body radiated in the sun while he coaxed her into the pool. He kept telling her how beautiful she was.

"I just really missed you, Georgia," he said.

"I'm not her."

"Georgia, did you get my letters?"

"Letters?"

"Yes, baby," he said. "Check the locked drawer."

"Locked drawer?" she asked.

"Yes. You told me you kept the key in the picture frame in one of the rooms, Georgia."

Dream Aliyah walked away from him.

"Stop it!" she exclaimed. "I don't know what you're talking about."

"Yes, you do. Read the letters."

Aliyah couldn't take it anymore. She did her best to wake up from the dream. It took a couple of tries, but she did it.

When she woke up, her shirt was wet and sticking to her. Her heart was beating fast, and she needed to calm down.

Thankful for the night lights in the house, she grabbed a cup from her cabinet and poured herself some water. It cooled her down. When finished, she changed her shirt. She was too afraid to go to sleep.

Aliyah was curious.

She went into both guest rooms to see which one had a piece of furniture with a locked drawer. When she found it, from there she took down each of her aunt's photos with a frame and placed them face down on the bed. She took the back out of each. She found a silver key in a picture of her aunt at a pool.

"Now this is getting weird," Aliyah stated while she shakily took the key out.

She went to the dresser her aunt had in the room, put it into the lock, and it fit perfectly. Her heart started beating fast as she opened the drawer.

Right on top was a raggedy sheet of paper. She was afraid if she touched it, she'd ruin it. She went to the bathroom and washed and dried her hands thoroughly. She carefully grasped the piece of paper and saw thin cursive.

She hoped she could read it. She placed the note closer to her face and read it.

My sweet Georgia. I hope this letter reaches you in high spirits. I know it's been a month since I've seen you last. The sweet taste of your nether regions is fading from my lips. I miss sneaking kisses while your brother isn't looking. I miss having you in my arms every day before you go to work.

Now Aliyah was confused. Her aunt had never married; who the fuck was this man? She continued to read.

I'd lose a week of wages just to bury my nether region into yours until you call my name over and over. How I wish your sticky body would cling to mine as my motions send you to bliss.

I hope your parents are ready. I want to ask for your hand in marriage.

Yours truly, Barnabas

It was Barnabas! From the dream.

Aliyah cleared her throat. The man had a way with words—she was hot and bothered.

She flipped to the back to see if there was more. And there was.

There was a note from her aunt to Barnabas saying she would lose a week of wages just to be in his arms. She said she wanted to suck his nether regions until he couldn't come no more. She said she wanted to call his name to the heavens even though they weren't married.

Aliyah's eyes got wide as she read how much of a freak her great-aunt was. She looked in the drawer and found another letter.

Except this one was addressed to her.

The young woman scrunched her eyebrows up,

grabbed the paper, and sat on the bed in the guest bedroom. This was juicy.

My dear Aliyah,

If you are reading this, I must now be deceased, and you inherited my house. My dad, your grandfather, and my cousins built this house for me. In hopes that one day I could share it with a husband of my own.

There's something I've hidden for years. You may not believe me dear, but what I'm saying is true. I once was supposed to marry a lover of mine – Barnabas. In the 60s, I met him at a juke joint one night. He wasn't from the area, but we were enthralled with each other. For several months, we stayed in contact. However, we always made love in this house.

Barnabas had a job out of the state and we sometimes only saw each other once a month. Unfortunately, my lover had an untimely death before he could ask my parents for my hand in marriage.

You won't believe me, but I had sex with Barnabas's spirit for thirty years. It's not something easy to explain. But all those years you and your sister heard bumps in the night. Or folks saying they saw a silhouette of a man in the windows, it was Barnabas.

"What the hell!" Aliyah exclaimed, taking a break from reading. "This is some type of white people shit. What person has sex with a ghost?"

She shook her head in disbelief and continued to read.

All I can say is this house comes with fringe benefits. You will have sex with Barnabas. I tried to avoid it, but I always enjoyed his loving. When he comes around, you'll know it. He'll reveal himself to only you. Just go with it. You won't be disappointed.

There's another key in this drawer. It opens a small chest in the closet. You'll enjoy what is inside.

Love auntie G.

Aliyah sat on the bed to digest everything. This was overwhelming. But her aunt never steered her in the wrong direction.

She found the other key, walked to the closet, and found the chest.

In the chest were old photos of her great-aunt and Barnabas. My goodness, he was a beautiful specimen, just like in her dreams. He and her aunt looked great together. She could see the love in their eyes. In some of the photos, she saw the lust.

The chest also had a few of her aunt's old dresses. She wasn't sure if she could fit them, but they were gorgeous.

Aliyah was still stunned. She didn't know what to think or do. Her aunt was getting her rocks off from a ghost for the last three decades. She wasn't sure if she should tell Tonya. Or ask her grandad about Barnabas.

He never really talked about his sister's suitors.

Aliyah wasn't sure she was ready to have sex with a spirit. In her dreams, he was so mysterious and alluring, but what about Jason?

Was this safe? Would Barnabas reveal himself when she least expected?

"This is about to be interesting," she said heading to the bathroom to start her day.

* * *

That night when she went to bed, she dreamt of Barnabas. *In the dream, they danced the night away in an empty room. She was even in one of her aunt's dresses.*

No one was there but them. When they sat down to rest, Barnabas started a conversation.

"I know I've been intruding on your dreams, but it's easier to reveal myself in your dreams. I'm sorry I showed my presence though."

"You did?" she inquired.

"When you were in bed with that man, I closed the window in anger."

She covered her mouth in realization.

"I was just envious that someone else was all over your body instead of me. And when you rub yourself with oil every night after your shower, I want your skin all over mine."

Aliyah started blushing.

"But I can touch you," she said.

"I'm solid. I'm only see-through when others are around."

His hand reached out for hers, and he kissed it. Her face got warm in embarrassment.

Barnabas stood up, reached for her hand again, and said, "Let's go somewhere else. Wake up. When you do, I'll be there. Don't be alarmed."

Aliyah was nervous. She was always told when the dead come to you in your dreams, don't go with them. They'll try to take you to your death. But something told her she could trust him.

She didn't want to wake up from the dream, but she did. When she came to her senses, she looked at the foot of her bed. He sat there, thankfully not looking at her, but he was taking his shoes off.

The moon's glow added an ambiance to the room, and before she knew it, Nina Simone's "I Put a Spell on You" lowly played.

"How did you do that?" she asked him.

"Don't worry about it," he said, standing up and reaching for her hand.

They were face to face, and she was in a trance.

His hands deftly unwrapped her dress from her body. The dress was like a puddle around her feet. She stood there beautifully in a black bra, black slip, and barefoot. Barnabas helped her step over her dress and wrapped his arms around her waist. They fit perfectly in a hug, and she couldn't help but nuzzle her face in the crook of his neck.

Her eyes closed in ecstasy at the embrace. He nuzzled his face in the crook of her neck, only to suck on her sensitive flesh. Her eyes rolled to the back of her head. She held on to him for balance.

Barnabas's hands rubbed all over her bottom. She felt her senses tingle as he squeezed both her ass cheeks.

His lips quit assaulting her neck and traveled up to her chin. When he took his lips in hers, she obliged. She couldn't believe how in sync their lips were. Her tongue asked for entrance into his mouth, and he allowed her in.

Moans escaped both of their mouths at the feeling. She couldn't believe it. A ghost was in the flesh in her house enticing her with a kiss. She removed her tongue from the kiss and came up for air.

"Undress me," he said. She wasted no time getting him naked. The moonlight was the perfect lighting for his body. She kissed him vigorously from the lips down to his abdomen and to his thighs.

She couldn't avoid the appendage in the middle of his legs. It hung there—low. It was thicker than a Snicker. The tip of it was the size of a golf ball. The veins looked like a design on the appendage.

He wasn't bothered when her small hands held his member. She kissed the length of it, and his head tilted back when she let the tip slide through her lips. He tried to control his breathing as her hands methodically worked it.

She placed her hands on his hips as she engulfed six of his eight inches in her mouth. She shimmied it in and out until he placed his hand on her head and let her face stay there as he face-fucked her.

Saliva left her lips and fell to the floor.

He removed his hand from her head and helped her to her feet as she caught her breath.

He wasted no time and led her to the bed, where he removed her bra, slip, and underwear.

Barnabas had his hands on her breasts. She moaned as he kissed her.

Her aunt's letter had said to go with the flow—and she was. Hell! Her pussy had a flow—she was getting wet just from his touch and kisses.

His appendage was still hard as a rock as she squirmed under him with his actions. He moved his hands from her breasts and rubbed her thighs as he kissed all over her face. He grabbed his appendage and slid the head over her folds. He let it "knock" on her clit, and her senses were on overload.

Barnabas let the golf ball-shaped head slide between her folds three times before putting all his length in. She did a soft gasp at the feel, and he hissed. His girth stretched her the right way.

He didn't move right away because he had to pace himself. It'd been almost a decade since he'd been with a woman.

He wanted to dance in her womanhood until she twirled into ecstasy. The movement was all in his hips as he swiveled them to the beat they'd created. His thrusts were long and soft—it was more sensual and romantic than the dancing in her dream.

Her breathing was becoming quicker. She managed to open her eyes and look up at him. His love faces were beautiful as he rolled, rocked, and grooved to give her this bedroom performance. Beads of sweat formed on his forehead as he concentrated on his strokes.

Barnabas grunted when he noticed with each stroke he gave, she thrust back at him. They did this for several beats until he pushed her knees into her chest as he pumped in and out of her rapidly.

Aliyah cheered him on as his thick member worked her nether region. The sloshing sounds of her pussy was music to his ears.

She could hear his breathing get faster as his strokes came closer together, and she knew he was about to come. She smiled because she knew his love face would be beautiful. The bed had the sweetest rhythm as it rocked on the wall to their passion. He groaned as he hit the pinnacle. His strokes slowed down. He took a final satisfied sigh, and she smirked as he came back to reality.

Aliyah smirked because she felt like the ultimate cheerleader getting him to that point. He kissed her on the lips and said, "Outstanding. Just like old times."

She was saddened a bit because she knew he was reminiscing about her Aunt Georgia. It hurt a little knowing she wasn't who he wanted her to be.

She looked down at the bedspread and said, "I'm not Georgia."

He used one hand to cup her chin. They looked into each other's eyes, and he said, "I know."

"You do?"

He nodded and said, "I'll explain how later. But right now, I want you on top of me."

And she squealed in excitement when he rolled her over and had her on top.

First Time
By L. Lawrence

"Rumor has it that Chris will be there tonight. And he is divorced," my best friend D'Asia said to me as she drove us to our high school reunion.

"Really?" I smirked as I looked out my window.

"Crazy ironic that you're both divorced," she continued. "It's fate!"

"Stop it, girl!" I laughed as she talked.

I can't lie, though. Upon hearing that Chris would be there, I had a couple of butterflies in my stomach.

Chris McFadden was my boyfriend my junior and senior year of high school. We graduated in 2002, but 2000 to 2002 were our dating years.

I've dated four men in my life. Out of the four of them, he was one of the top tier men.

I hoped he hadn't changed.

Chris was sweet and caring. The exact opposite of my ex-husband Malcolm.

Malcolm and Chris were both intelligent beings, but Malcolm was bitter and cold.

"Nia." D'Asia said my name. "Are you going to speak to Chris?"

"Hell yeah!" I told her. "Chris and I broke up on mutual terms."

We broke up in the summer of 2002. We were going to two different colleges in the same state, but we thought it was best.

The older women in my life told me to be single my freshman year of college. I'm glad I listened.

My freshmen year was amazing! I was in different activities at the college, went on a few dates, but I didn't feel tied down like some of my girlfriends.

Even though I went on a few dates, my mind still lingered on Chris McFadden. We would talk occasionally over the years, but nothing romantic.

"What are you thinking about?" D'Asia asked me.

"I'm just thinking about how I met Malcolm and our marriage. He really had me fooled," I told her.

"He had a lot of us fooled," she stated.

"Don't get me wrong. He was legit, yet he had some things to work on."

I met Malcolm in 2010. I was 26 and he was 29. We both had decent jobs. I was a manager at Walmart, and he was in real estate. He happened to get into it when the nation was turning things around after the housing crash.

I saw some red flags in him the first year we were together, but it's like they faded into pink flags as time went on.

We married in 2012 but divorced in 2015. We have a beautiful son together. I prayed Malcolm and I could work things out, but he was a narcissist. He had a power complex, and I couldn't deal with it.

It would be unhealthy for me and our son.

D'Asia knew about it. She helped me leave safely. Malcolm would physically push me, hold my arms and wrists tightly to control me, and there were two instances where he tried to hit me.

That was the final straw. I needed to leave before things worsened.

I'd been single the last seven years. I'd been dating since 2021, but I would love to date Chris again to see if we were still a great match. I was a different person than 18-year-old me. I was sure the same was true for him.

And my goodness the sex was beautiful. We didn't know much about sex back then, but we were each other's firsts. Hell! I still remembered our first time. It was awkward at first, but the rest of the night was like a sweet dream.

We were originally supposed to have sex prom night our senior year, but we were having so much fun that night being with our friends. We were on the dance floor the majority of the night. Our limousine drove us around the city. We were too tired to try sex that night.

But my goodness! Our graduation night was a night to remember. My mom used her sewing machine for weeks to create a pink and silver dress for me. I wore it underneath my cap and gown.

Chris wore a white button shirt and black slacks with his cap and gown. He and my mom were in cahoots with each other because the pink she used for my dress, she had sewn pink cuffs on his button-down.

The McFaddens had a small graduation party at their house for Chris. My parents had a bigger gradua-tion party for me at a hotel downtown.

While my family members cleaned up, my older cousin took me and my friends home. Except when she dropped me off at my house, Chris was with me. We had the whole house to ourselves.

D'Asia had decorated my room. It was nothing extravagant, but she cleaned it and bought scented candles. There was a small box of condoms next to my bed. There were hearts sprinkled all over the floor and bed.

Chris was shocked!

"We're doing this tonight?" he inquired.

"Do you not want to?" I asked in a nervous tone.

I was starting to feel foolish.

I thought he wanted to have sex with me. What if he didn't want to have sex with me? What if he wanted a more experienced woman?

"Oh trust me. I do," he admitted. "But you told me we were going to break up this summer. So I thought it meant we weren't going to fuck."

"We have the whole summer to figure that out. Right now I just want to experience this with you and no one else."

Chris grinned big! Before I knew it, he picked me up and tossed me on my bed. I couldn't help squealing.

He started taking his clothes off and rushed through getting mine off. I was used to seeing him shirtless, but I had never seen his dick before. I'd always only felt it. It hung downwards.

It was cold in the room, and it felt weird being completely naked around him. I wrapped my arms around myself.

The most I'd ever been around him was in a bra and jeans or shorts.

My breasts have always been on the small. I've been called skinny since the eighth grade, but Chris didn't seem to care.

He unwrapped my arms and held me in a tight embrace as his lips kissed mine. I started to warm up at this familiar gesture. My arms wrapped around his body naturally. While he kissed me, his hands snaked down to my thighs. He carefully slipped my legs apart and used one finger inside me.

"Ow!" I said. "What the hell was that?"

"I'm trying to finger you."

"Baby. No. Not like this," I said.

I curved my fingers in my mouth and started rubbing on my coochie lips. I'd never had sex, but I'd definitely fingered myself before.

"Ohhh," he said as I removed my fingers.

He looked down at my coochie and licked between the folds a bit. It felt a little weird to have hot flesh down there. He removed his mouth and rubbed on my coochie. He slowly slid one finger in there, and it felt good.

He kissed me as he did this. I moaned from the stimulation. This didn't last long because he placed my hand on his hammer. It was hot, sticky, and wet. My hand stroked it up and down. He watched me as I did it.

His dick was quite thick and had length. I was nervous about that thing going inside of me.

"Fuck, Nia," he whispered as I spit on it so my hand could twist easily.

I watched and felt as his dick got harder in my hand. I was ready to have him inside of me.

"Do you want me to stop so we can get something to eat?"

"Huh?"

"You want me to stop so we can eat?" D'Asia inquired.

That ruined my flashback. She was pulling off an exit to get gas. A few food spots were nearby.

We were 30 minutes from our destination. But I wanted to eat because the event started in three hours, and I was hungry.

I was horny too. But my best friend didn't need to know this.

We found a fast food joint to sit in and ordered our food. We were both mothers. So she checked in on her kids, and I checked in on my son.

After the call, we ate, sat, and wondered who would be at the reunion.

We settled back into the car. Even though we were close to our destination, I still managed to fall asleep.

I dreamt of my first time with Chris.

Our foreplay back then didn't last long. I remember him grabbing a condom and putting it on.

"I want you to sit on it," he said, lying on my pillows and trying to get me on top of him.

"What?" I asked him. "On top? Are you crazy?"

"It'll be easier."

"I ain't never heard of a woman giving away her virginity by being on top."

"My cousin said he and his girl did it that way. And it worked for her."

My heart started to beat fast because every girl I knew said they did it on their back. Some said it hurt. Others said it was just fine. But I didn't want to do this on top.

It didn't sound normal.

I expected the pain. I expected a little blood. But being on top—I wasn't expecting that.

"We already have a nice ambiance in the room. I'll play some music. We'll keep the mood going, but I think this might be the move. It won't hurt you."

I looked in his eyes, and I'm sure he could tell I was nervous. I felt like I was ruining everything by being a punk.

"Let me put on music," he said, getting out of bed.

He found the mix CD we'd burned for prom night. He placed it in my radio.

The first track on the list was "Full Moon" by Brandy.

He climbed back in the bed, motioned me to him, and said, "Spit on it."

I spat on the condom, he used his fingers to lubricate it, and then he used both hands to cup my butt cheeks.

"I'm just as nervous as you," he said. "But it looks good in here. You look good. Your favorite singer is singing."

I started smiling.

Chris pulled me closer to his lips. He sloppily kissed me, but I didn't mind. His hands rubbed over my butt, and it felt good.

Chris deserved a kisser of the year award because his kisses had me melting like hot candle wax.

I wasn't sure when he did it, but I felt the head of his hammer sliding up and down my slit. My eyes rolled to the back of my head at the feeling.

He wasn't even inside of me yet, and I could hear the wetness of my pussy. I held on to his chest for balance as the head knocked at my entrance a few times. I looked in his eyes as his hand guided his dick to do the same combinations over. The sliding through my slit, the head knock, then back to the sliding, and finally, the head slipped past my coochie lips.

I didn't tense up as I thought I would. He glided right through my coochie. I heard and felt a gush of air hit my punani.

"Fuck!" he uttered. I didn't realize it then, but I'm sure being inside of a girl was a different feeling. It was his first time inside punani.

"I won't move," he said, looking in my eyes. His hands were still gripping my butt.

"I'll slide you up and down a few times."

He did it slowly, and I breathed my way through it

those first ten seconds. It did not take long for my eyes to close in bliss.

It must have felt good to him too because I heard him grunting.

We were in sync, and I was confident in myself. I used my knees to bounce on him. I felt like my legs were flapping like an eagle's wings. My thighs were burning like I had just finished jump roping.

I tried to work through the pain in my thighs, but I heard him whimpering softly. He grabbed my apple bottom again and changed my strokes to what he needed. I looked in his face and his face was twisted in a grimace.

Chris looked goofy as hell. Now that I'm experienced, I understand he hit his climax. He was only in me for five minutes.

He kissed me on my lips and carefully pulled me off of him.

My coochie didn't hurt. My thighs were still vibrating.

After he threw the rubber away, he rushed to my side asking me if I was okay.

I explained to him I was fine. It was easier than I thought. But my thighs were a different story.

While I checked the bed for sheets, he ran me a hot bath in the hallway bathroom. I didn't stay in it long. I just needed my thighs to calm down. I was thankful I didn't bleed everywhere.

While I dried off, I told him I wanted to try one more time.

"Are you up to it?" he asked.

"Yes. I want to before my folks get home."

We walked to my bed and slid into it. He started kissing me like his life depended on it. His large hands covered my slender body, and he kneaded my breasts. I don't know how, but it made me feel warm all over. He stopped to stroke himself, and it was fascinating to watch. He grabbed another condom, and I watched as he put it on. He spit on my punani.

This time I watched as his joystick made its way to my coochie. He slipped the tip in and pulled out—twice. He entered a little more, and I winced.

"You want me to stop?" he asked.

"No," I whispered. I probably should have stayed in the bath a little longer.

His strokes were slow and purposeful. My legs were wide open for him. I wanted to stay in this position with him forever. It was just us home, no rush. I had no need to be quiet. My twin-sized bed rattled underneath us making love. This moment was made for me and him, and I didn't regret it.

"You're so fucking pretty," he murmured in between kissing me. He remained in eye contact with me, but I closed my eyes in embarrassment. Then I started making noise straight out of porn. My heart

rate was increasing. My body was warm all over. I had to hold on to him and the pillow next to me for balance.

My eyes closed tightly, and there was a wave of pleasure coating my insides as I came on his hammer. I didn't scream, but I whimpered like a baby. He didn't stop, but continued to give me a few more slow strokes. Then I felt a calm wash over me, and I slowly opened my eyes to see a smiling Chris.

I think I only lasted for three minutes, but who cares?

He pulled out of me and threw the rubber away. We lay naked in my bed. He held me in his arms, and I felt so loved. We started to doze to sleep until my cousin called my room phone. She told me my parents were on their way home.

Chris and I got rid of every piece of evidence—the condoms, the candles, and him. I even washed my sheets.

He kissed me before leaving.

"If I could, I'd stay the night with you," he said.

"Girl! We at my mama's house. Wipe your drool and get out the car!" D'Asia told me.

"Huh?" I mumbled. "We're at my mom's. Let's greet her so we can get ready."

While I was sad my flashback was over, once I came to my senses, I was more than ready to see Chris tonight.

After we spent an hour chatting with D'Asia's mom, we took showers in the two different bathrooms.

Tonight I was going to wear an emerald long-sleeve dress that came to my ankles. My accessories would be gold. My pumps were gold. My hair was in three stitch braids that had bouncy curls at the end. I had gained a little weight over the last few years, but in the right places. I had more hip and dips now. My breasts weren't so small anymore.

When we arrived at the venue for the reunion, there was a red carpet rolled out for us alumni. There were two photographers outside snapping photos of us. This felt lavish.

We walked inside, and everyone was having a great time.

My heart was starting to beat fast because what if Chris was here. He posted on Facebook like six times a year. I wasn'tsure how he looked now.

D'Asia and I walked around and saw some familiar faces. There was a small memorial wall with pictures of teachers that had died since our graduation. As well as a few classmates we lost.

I was grabbing myself a mojito from the buffet of drinks when I heard someone belt out my name.

"Nia Francis. You haven't aged since 2002," the man said.

I carefully turned around and saw T.J. James. I did

my best not to roll my eyes. He'd been wanting my honey pot since we were in middle school. He still looked good, but he was annoying.

And he wasn't Chris.

We sparked a small conversation. He's doing well in life. He seems happy. Which was good because he had a traumatic year our junior year of high school—something straight out of *20/20*.

D'Asia came to save me and we went on to see a few other former classmates. I scanned the room to see if I saw Chris, but no success.

Thirty minutes into the event, I was tired of dancing. D'Asia came to me and said, "Let's eat."

We made ourselves a small plate and ate at the bar tables set up for us.

I was in the middle of stuffing fried mac and cheese balls in my mouth when a man approached.

"D'Asia and Nia always knew how to eat good and look good while doing it!"

The man chuckled.

We both wiped our mouths clean as we tried to recognize the voice. When we glanced up, we saw it was Chris.

He and D'Asia joked with each other like how they used to.

Me, on the other hand, I couldn't stop looking at him. He had a nice salt and pepper curly afro. No beard, no mustache, but he was still on the slender side. He had on a tailored suit. His arms looked like they wanted to bust out of the jacket.

His skin was free of blemishes, and he smelled great!

After they finished laughing, his attention was set on me. He licked his bottom lip and said, "You look beautiful, Nia."

"You look beyond handsome," I told him. "Are you enjoying the night?"

"I wasn't at first, but now that I see you, I know I will."

I smiled at him.

"Nia. This is my first time seeing you in years. How have you been?"

Power Play
By Shea Watts

Nuevo. Nuut. Novo. Yeni. In different languages, that's how one can say the word *new*.

New.

Tasha's husband, Vince, told her a month ago that he wanted to try something new and different in the bedroom.

She loved his honesty because it was the reason they have been married for so long. The two met in college and married when they were 21. Now they were 28, and he wanted more of a power play in the bedroom.

They're both really driven and killing it in their jobs. He's a lawyer, and she's a college professor–but the spark has gone out of their sex life.

For the last few weeks, she has been trying different things, and he actually liked it. They have experienced sex in the dark and with the lights on. They always had sex in the bed, on their dresser, or in their shower. But recently it's been the kitchen table or in the car.

However, Vince has asked for her to be more dominating.

Which is why she was currently at her kitchen table on her laptop doing research. He would be home from work soon, and she was researching how to be a dominatrix. The woman was always a book nerd, so this was fun to research.

She was in awe that this type of role was more than leather outfits and whips. The gamuts included consent, boundaries, safe words, and setting the scene.

Tasha was focused and fascinated. This was about to be interesting.

* * *

"It's so dark this morning," Tasha grumbled.

It was a Tuesday morning, and her alarm went off to start the morning.

"Stay in bed with me," Vince groggily whispered in her ear.

It took a minute for her to realize what was going on, but she was currently the little spoon. His one arm was wrapped around her torso, and his dick was hard —pressed on her ass.

"Let me take your shorts off of you and give you Mr. Jimmy," he said, referring to his dick.

She was thankful her husband couldn't see her sly smile because they needed to stay centered. They both had to get ready for work. But she really wanted him inside of her. She didn't care if he was in her mouth or pussy—she wanted him.

On the other hand, one of them had to be responsible.

"We don't have time," she told him.

"I'll make it quick," he murmured in her ear as he rubbed on her stomach and ass.

"We're never quick though," she told him.

"I don't care if I nut or not. I'm hard as hell," he said, placing her free hand on Mr. Jimmy.

Tasha gave in to Vince, and he fucked her until she had a small climax. Her body trembled and hummed afterward. When she and Vince shared a shower to make themselves so fresh and clean, her body was still humming.

She couldn't stop admiring his physique. Vince has a light skin complexion. His arms and abdomen were very firm and tight. His thighs could probably open a watermelon. But the way she admired him, he constantly admired her.

Her skin tone was darker than his. Her breasts were on the heavier side, she had a muffin top, and her ass was the shape of the perfect peach.

They couldn't keep their hands off each other as they dressed. She couldn't stop smiling on her way to the college.

Vince even texted her when she got to work about how sexy and spicy their morning was.

Her eyes fluttered closed as she thought about the experience. Then it hit her unexpectedly, she had a lightbulb moment for her and her husband.

Tonight she was going on an online shopping spree.

* * *

"Babe!" Vince yelled from downstairs. "You have a few packages," he said while bringing the boxes inside.

Tasha grinned wickedly as she stood at the top of the stairs. Vince walked up the steps and passed them to her.

"It's Thursday night. Our date night," he said. "Is one of those boxes something for date night?"

"Not quite," she yelled from the second floor. "But close."

Vince looked at her with his, "What are you up to?" face.

"I bet the suspense is killing you, isn't it?" she said to him.

"Yes. But I trust you. It looks like you know what you're doing."

"Thanks, babe."

She carried the boxes to their room and locked the door. These boxes contained two types of ropes, blindfolds, a pair of scissors, and a paddle for the night she was going to do her power play with him.

Tonight she was going to take time to try the items out on herself. When she researched BDSM topics, different websites voiced the importance of utilizing props on oneself before using them with a partner.

She bought a silk rope and tied one of her ankles to the bottom of the bedpost. She had the grip too tight but loosened it. She hoped Vince liked to be tied up. The scissors were there to cut the rope.

Then she tried the paddle on her pillow. Then on herself and said, "Ow!"

That was too rough.

"I'll make sure not to go so hard on hubby."

She used the next 15 minutes to try out each item on herself a few times. Then she cleaned up and tucked everything in the box under the bed.

It was Friday evening, and Tasha was ready to unwind. It was going on 3 p.m., and she emailed her students that no after-school help was available today. She wanted to go home and be under her husband. When she got home, Vince wasn't there yet.

She put everything work related away and grabbed herself a bottle of wine. She was going to finish the bottle by the time Vince got home.

When he walked in around 4:45 p.m. she was excited to see him.

"Hey, baby," he said, hugging her tight. He peppered kisses all over her face. "You look comfortable," he stated, looking at her relaxed.

"You look fine as hell in your suit," she told him.

"You know I have to look good for the court," he said, heading upstairs.

"Come join me," she told him. "There's another bottle in the fridge."

"Say less!" he exclaimed from the second floor.

For the next three hours, they had a blast doing nothing. They drank wine and watched movies.

Vince couldn't lie. There was nowhere else in the world he wanted to be.

They were about to start their third movie when their Ring Doorbell went off.

"I ordered something," she said.

"Again?" he asked her. "I need to call you Package Princess. What you got?"

"I can't tell you. It's a surprise."

He laughed.

"This better be a good surprise. You have been secretive these last few days."

"I'm just trying something different," she said.

Tasha went to the door and grabbed her package.

As she walked upstairs, all she could think to herself was, "If only Vince knew that I'm going to give him an out-of-body experience with all these packages."

The couple enjoyed the rest of their night and fell asleep after eating dinner and watching movies.

The next morning when she woke up, Vince was not in bed. It smelled so good in the house. He must have cooked. She was hoping to cuddle with him, but she went into the bathroom to start her morning hygiene routine.

When she went back into the bedroom, he had trays of food on the nightside table.

He was shirtless in his gray basketball shorts. She bit her bottom lip as he helped her get back in the bed.

He could feel her eyes on him, and he said, "Calm down, horny woman. I'd rather we eat breakfast instead of you trying to jump my bones."

"I'm sorry," she joked. "I'm practicing being dominant for our future sexcapades."

"Well, you're doing an outstanding job," he said passing her a tray of food.

"This looks amazing," she said, pleased with the food as he grabbed his tray.

He made pancakes with turkey sausage, sliced apples, and there was a small dipping container with peanut butter. He made them glasses of orange juice.

"Would you be comfortable if I tied you to the bed during sex?" she asked.

"Huh?" he asked, pouring syrup over his pancakes.

"Would you be comfortable if I tied you to the bed during sex?" she repeated.

"Yes, babe. You can. You all right?" he asked her with a side-eye.

"I'm fine," she said, taking mental notes.

"Do you give me consent to paddle you?" she asked.

"Tasha. What?" he asked.

"Answer the question, Vince."

"Yes," he told her. "But my safe word is *bug*."

"What? How did you come up with that?"

"Because apple and banana is too common. Besides, bug will make anyone stop. It's only one syllable."

"What are your plans for today?" she inquired.

"Don't change the subject," he told his wife. "I can even tell you're taking mental notes. What are you up to, wife?"

"Good trouble," she said before stuffing pancakes in her mouth.

Vince continued to look at his wife in awe.

"What are your plans for today?" she repeated.

"The guys and I are going to play basketball later today. But I should be back home by 6 p.m. You?"

"I have papers to grade. Then I'm catching up on my shows."

"It seems like a lowkey day," he said, digging into his pancakes.

"Thank goodness," she said. "I need to rest up."

As the day went on, the couple finished breakfast, cleaned up after themselves, and around three, he left to go hoop with the fellas.

When he came back around 6, he showered, and she was still grading papers in the bedroom.

He told her he was going to take a nap downstairs.

"Please wake me up by 7:30," he said.

"I got you baby. Go rest up."

She finished her work, put a meal in the crock pot, and went upstairs to shower.

When she came out of the shower and dried off, she rubbed her African Royale Hot Six Oil over her breasts, under them, over her stomach, and down her thighs.

She looked in the mirror and loved how radiant the

oil made her skin. The light fragrance of the oil always made Vince flock to her.

Tasha walked to her bedroom closet and grabbed the leather outfit that had been delivered to her yesterday.

Tonight was the night.

The red leather corset came with matching underwear, but she didn't waste her time putting it on. She knew once Vince saw and smelled her, Mr. Jimmy would be at attention.

She took her time putting on the corset and a pair of black stilettos. The rope, scissors, paddle, and blindfolds fit into a small, cute bookbag. She carefully walked downstairs to see Vince on the sofa knocked out.

She snickered lowly. Tasha placed the bag on the floor.

Then she walked to Vince and gently shook his shoulders.

"Baby. Wake up," she said.

He mumbled and rolled over onto his side.

She did the same gesture again to try and wake him.

"All right, babe," he mumbled.

She chuckled because she knew he was about to fall back asleep.

She needed to kill some time.

Her high heels clickety-clacked on their hardwood floor as she walked into the kitchen to check on their crockpot meal.

She walked back to him and said, "Wake up sleepyhead."

He smiled at her sweet voice. Then rolled onto his back.

She took this as her cue to crawl on top of him.

His eyes fluttered open due to her movements.

She laid her head on his chest.

"What's up, cutie?" he asked, enjoying the warmth of her body on him.

"Waiting for you to wake up so we can have quality time together tonight."

"Quality time sounds great," he said, rubbing one hand up and down her back.

"What the hell?" he mumbled, feeling the texture of her corset.

He had no clue what his wife was wearing, but it was different than the usual cotton pieces she wore. He was curious now.

"Tasha. Sit up," he said in a curious tone.

The dark-skinned woman carefully removed herself from her husband's body and stood before him. She even did a 360 degree turn to show her outfit.

He whistled and howled at the sight of her.

"Damn. That's a woman right there!" he said, admiring her.

Vince wanted to stuff his face in between her breasts. Her skin glistened and looked so soft. He wanted to lick every nook and cranny of her.

She didn't have underwear on, and he wanted to bend her over the sofa and nut in her until it leaked out of her.

She bent over to pick up the bag of goodies, and he smacked her ass.

Tasha's face got warm from him giving her attention.

"This bag contains items that will make tonight memorable."

He raised his eyebrows up at his wife.

"You are such a nerd," he said, standing up to hug her. "But you're my sexy nerd."

"I won't be your nerd tonight," she said, getting out of his grasp.

She pulled the paddle out of the bag and said, "Take your ass upstairs before I spank you with this."

"Oh shit!" he exclaimed.

"Now go upstairs and freshen up before I give you this pussy," she said, following him up there.

Vince did just that and met her in the bedroom. He was naked.

"Lay on the bed like you are about to do a snow angel!" she instructed.

He spread his legs and arms wide. He was taken aback when he saw his wife take the rope from her book bag.

She had been practicing knots the last few days and tied the rope around his ankles.

"You good?" she asked.

"It's not too tight," he said, enjoying her being out of her element.

She cut the rope where she saw fit and then tied his non-dominant hand to the headboard. She needed one of his hands to be her scrunchie.

She moved the scissors and rope back to the bag and pulled out a blindfold for him. Then put the bag on the floor.

Vince started laughing.

"A blindfold too. Damn, baby. You just have all of these plans, don't you?"

She laughed back as she placed the blindfold on his eyes. She knew he was laughing with her, not at her.

"Damn, skippy," she said.

She pulled her hair out of her face and looked at Mr. Jimmy. He was getting hard, and she was gonna finish the job.

She slid between Vince's legs and grabbed Mr. Jimmy. She tapped his head on her bottom lip, and it was heavy. She slid Mr. Jimmy into her mouth slowly, and Vince nodded his head back.

He let out a shallow breath as his wife attacked his tip with her mouth. Her hand did a twisting motion up and down his shaft.

"Mr. Jimmy said don't be shy and put all of him in your mouth."

Vince's eyes rolled to the back of his head while all of him filled her warm mouth.

She let Mr. Jimmy hit the back of her throat until she couldn't breathe. The spit dangled from her mouth when she released her husband's penis.

While she caught her breath, her hands stroked Mr. Jimmy from top to bottom.

Tasha wanted to drive Vince wild. She sucked on Mr. Jimmy's head as she stroked the length of him. She made sure to do variations of sucking on the mushroom-shaped tip before finally making her cheeks hollow and sucking hard on the sensitive piece.

Due to the blindfold, Vince couldn't see her, but he was sure he had to pull her hair away from her face. He used one hand to hold her hair from her face. It helped her perform better. It was like her mouth and hand were working like a machine to make him nut all over her.

She could hear Vince's pants come closer together.

"I'm finna nut," he said.

The woman pulled Mr. Jimmy out of her mouth to regulate her breathing. She wasted no time stroking him a little faster and then sucking the tip.

"Fuck!" she heard her husband grunt as his salty and hot nut entered her mouth. She did her best to swallow, but he placed his free hand on the top of her head. He pushed Mr. Jimmy deeper in her mouth to make his climax last longer.

She felt his body convulse around her.

When he couldn't take it anymore, he removed himself from her mouth that was like a warm pot of water.

Tasha swallowed his nut. She was pleased with how she handled him. He didn't come from head often, so it was refreshing to see this occur.

Her pussy was starting to water from their actions.

Vince asked for the rope to be moved to his other hand.

Tasha did what he asked—anything to make him comfortable.

She told him to eat her pussy.

"Hell, yeah," he said.

Before he knew it, she was sitting on his face.

Mr. Jimmy jumped from this.

The woman relished in the feeling of his warm tongue muscle inside her pussy. She just needed head to prepare herself for Mr. Jimmy.

She slid off her husband's face and came face to face with Mr. Jimmy again. She kissed the muscle that was now getting soft. Vince's body quivered at the feeling.

It didn't take her long to get him hard again. She had Mr. Jimmy so wet, she was wet, and she was ready to slide down him. She hovered over her husband's lower half, grabbed Mr. Jimmy, and slid down him like a stripper slides down a pole.

Vince cussed in pleasure because she was not playing games. She usually let her pussy adjust to Mr. Jimmy, but she moved instantly on him.

Tasha was creating the perfect momentum for them. He couldn't see her, but he could imagine how she looked. He was sure the red leather corset still made her look curvy. Her hair was probably a mop over her head. Based on her moans, he was positive her love faces were sexy as hell too.

Shit! He only been in her for a few moments, and he felt like he was going to blow his load. He felt like Tasha was a rock star and he was a fan. He enjoyed just lying there to enjoy her pussy lips not letting him go.

The different strokes she was giving him had him tossing and turning in the bed. Her pussy had him in gridlock. Sex with his wife had always been amazing. But tonight, she was really on to something with this power play. He was stuck like Gorilla Glue—he didn't budge as she rolled her hips to perform for him.

Hell! She was gently tugging on his nipples while riding. She didn't do that often, and it felt great to him.

He had to hold on tight to the bedspread. He usually didn't show the love faces he made, but tonight was different.

Vince was trying to maintain his pace and not come so fast, but the grip her pussy had on him didn't allow that to happen.

He was close to nutting. His senses were enhanced because of the blindfold. He used his free hand to smack her ass. Then he held her in a position where he could just ram in her. It only took five heavy strokes before he released himself in her.

She knew he was spent when his arm fell to the bed.

Tasha kept going because she was about to release on him. This only made his orgasm last longer. He wanted to pull her off of him, but he knew she was close.

And it didn't take her long to come undone on Mr. Jimmy. Vince mustered enough strength to pump Mr. Jimmy in her longer while she hit her climax. The noise she made from her orgasm was like music to his ears. When she couldn't take it anymore, she collapsed on his chest—both of them with perspiration all over them.

When the adrenaline in Tasha calmed down, she got off his dick, grabbed the scissors, and took the ropes off him.

When his hand was released, he wasted no time taking the blindfold off. He pulled his wife on top of him.

"Come here woman!" he exclaimed. He kissed her lips nasty and slow. "It's been a while since we had something this intimate! Shit! What else you got for me?"

She released herself from his grip and grabbed the paddle.

"I command you to take my corset off of me."

He moved too slowly for her liking, and she hit his ass with the paddle.

Vince looked at Tasha. Tasha looked at Vince. They busted out laughing.

But he looked at her in her eyes and coyly said, "Do more of that."

Tasha was shocked her husband wanted more of this. But this was the power play he wanted. She used the paddle on the lower part of his butt, and hearing his small wince made her smile.

Vince took off the corset, and he sucked her nipples.

He wanted to ravish her body. He licked, sucked, and bit all over her body, and she writhed in pleasure at how well he was taking care of her body.

"What do you want to do next madam?"

She said, "Make love to me while we have the blindfolds on."

"Can I put the rope around your wrists?" he asked her.

"Yes," she consented.

He bound her wrists in front of her. He grabbed the blindfolds and put them on her and himself.

He used his fingers to pull her chin closer to his and kissed her until she was on her back and he was on top of her. He wasted no time eating her pussy again, and she sang her praises to him. He listened to her instructions when she said, "Don't stop."

She was about to come when he stopped.

He laid them on their side and nasty talked in her ear.

"I'm gonna make love to you until your gushy pussy makes the bedspread wet. You are so mother-fucking sexy, and I want to bury myself in you."

Him whispering in her ear was a turn-on. Because of her hands being tied in rope she couldn't push him off. But she didn't want to really push him off anyway. She felt Mr. Jimmy's head sliding on her folds. Vince was teasing her with Mr. Jimmy, and she said, "Put him in all ready."

And he did what he was told to do. They both did a satisfied sigh when he made it inside her.

He used Mr. Jimmy to bring her to ecstasy. His movements were smooth, sensual and made her feel like she was floating in a dream. He was so glad her hands were bound. He used his fingers to stimulate her clit as he passionately made love to her.

Tasha just lay there and enjoyed the feelings. His actions were getting her closer to the final destination of her dream.

"Don't hold it in, baby," he said.

She wanted to use her hands to swat his fingers away but couldn't. But she sucked it up and took Mr. Jimmy like a professional. Her body convulsed, and she squirted on their bedspread as she climaxed.

It pushed Mr. Jimmy out. So Vince removed his fingers from her clit and reinserted Mr. Jimmy.

"Oh my God," she shouted. "Oh my God."

"Bug!" she exclaimed. "Bug!"

He pulled out.

"Are you okay?" he asked. He remembered the safe word.

He grabbed the scissors and snipped the rope around her wrists.

"I'm fine. It was just overly stimulating."

He laughed.

"Thank goodness. I was worried I went over-board," he said, releasing her from the bondage.

"Baby. That was amazing! We need to do this more often."

"You took the words right out of my mouth," he said, kissing her.

Game Time
By Carmen Summerlin

It was football Sunday. Laila and Damian were pumped for their Sunday routine with friends.

Laila knew Damian was going to go all-out for the food. He was making cheesy bread, wings, homemade guac, and tortilla chips.

His friends Greg and Tavon were coming over. She was excited for them to come over because they were a solid set of guys.

Tavon was nerdy like Damian, but Greg was the more outgoing friend in the group.

The game was going to start at 3, but it was 1, and he was getting the cooking out of the way. She watched Damian while he put the chicken wings in the air fryer. He left about two dozen to the side because he wanted to fry those when the fellas arrived.

Damian was an attractive man on any given day,

but seeing him in the kitchen made him even more attractive. Damian had height, arms like a basketball player, and his almond eyes were the icing on the cake for his look.

"I can feel your eyes on me," Damian told Laila, his girlfriend of three years.

"I'm just watching you cook. I cook so much, I forgot you know how to cook," she told him.

"Hardy har har," he told his girlfriend. "And why are you wearing lounge-around clothes? Put on your outfit."

"My bad," she said, looking at her holey shirt and Clorox-stained basketball shorts. "Let me change."

She went to their bedroom to get dressed.

Today the Patriots and Giants were going against each other. Like Damian, she wasn't on team Giants or Patriots. She just enjoyed being around Damian.

She was wearing a split jersey shirt and jeans. The shirt had the Giants' and Patriots' mascots on it. She smeared some lip gloss on her lips and took photos to upload to Insta later.

Laila went back into the kitchen to help Damian.

"I wanna fuck you while you wear that," he said.

"I bet you do," she said. "But you know I have to conserve my energy today."

Damian snorted, "Energy."

Laila always had energy.

Damian bit his bottom lip as he watched her maneuver around the kitchen and decided to leave her alone. Because he knew today was going to be a long day for them.

One o'clock turned into two o'clock. Two o'clock quickly turned to 2:45, and then the boys arrived at the door.

Laila opened the door for them and let them in. They came in with beers and more bags of chips.

"Game day!" Greg's voice boomed as he placed the beers in the kitchen. His locs were piled up on his head.

Tavon came into the kitchen with more chips and a buffalo chicken dip. The waves in his hair would make any woman seasick.

Greg was in his Giants attire, while Tavon was in his Patriots attire.

"We all look good, family," Greg said, checking out everyone's fit.

"We gotta stay fly," Laila said to the boys. "And y'all best believe we're taking photos now."

The guys groaned, but they know Laila loved taking pictures. They posed with her for photos. While she uploaded the photos to Insta, the men started making their plates of food.

Laila noticed they didn't have their drinks, so she grabbed them all beers—two beers a piece.

The men got comfortable on the three-seater with their food.

After she passed them the drinks, she stood in front of the television and stripped out of her shirt and jeans.

Tavon and Greg dropped their jaws while looking at her.

Her green and white polka dot bikini fit well on her sculpted body. The men knew she went to the gym four days a week and watched how she ate, but damn it was doing her body great!

Laila was shaped like a video vixen. Her breasts sat pretty in the polka-dotted top, and her ass fit into the bikini bottom perfectly. She had no stomach. She was portioned very well. Her hair was in burgundy and black box braids that stopped at her collarbone.

Tavon couldn't lie. He wanted to smack her ass.

"So you two weren't joking," he said, looking between Laila and Damian.

"We were dead-ass serious," Damian said. "I cannot keep up with her sexual appetite."

It was hard for Damian to admit, but it was the truth. They typically had sex at least three days a week, but with her—she wanted sex five times a week. And sometimes she can go multiple times a day. It was a lot on his body.

They are always trying new adventures and challenges in their relationship, but for today Damian came up with a plan.

Damian was going to share Laila with Greg and Tavon.

"I'm wildly excited about this," Laila said. "Today I'm catering to all of you. I'm fine. You're not demeaning me. I'm okay with this."

"Remind me," Greg said. "What will the lovely lady be doing for us today?"

"If the Giants are ahead at halftime, Greg, I have to suck your dick," Laila said.

Tavon cleared his throat.

"If the Patriots are ahead at halftime, you have to give me head?"

Laila licked her bottom lip before telling Tavon, "Exactly that."

Greg and Tavon side-eyed Damian as Laila got comfortable on the loveseat.

"Don't forget," she told the fellas as she laid on the plush pillows on the chair. "Whichever team wins, I fuck the fan."

Damian grabbed the food from the kitchen to put in the den. What he didn't know was that Greg and Tavon texted each other about how crazy Damian was about sharing his girlfriend with them.

Everyone was tuned in as the kickoff occurred, but

during the first commercial break, Greg asked for a cigar.

Laila's ass moved like jam as she grabbed the cigar box and the lighter. She passed him his cigar and sat on his lap as she lit the cigar.

She did the same for Damian and Tavon, but Tavon made sure to smack her ass when she was on his lap.

"Do it again," she told him.

He didn't hesitate when he did it again. All she did was laugh with joy.

Each commercial break she did something to each guy. She would make sure her titties stayed in their faces, she sat on their laps, gave them lap dances, and she would wrap their arms around her body.

One commercial break, she sat in Greg's lap. She didn't object whenever he rubbed her back, thighs, or apple bottom.

When halftime came, the Patriots were up by two. Tavon stood up and cheered for his team. He was proud of how well the Patriots were performing.

He forgot about the deal.

Until he saw Laila put a pillow on the floor in front of him.

She unbuttoned the jeans and pulled them down to his ankle. He passed Greg his beer and pulled down his boxers.

Laila got on her knees. Thankful the pillow was there as a cushion.

Tavon's dick lay on display for her. He looked down at her as she wasted no time placing her warm hand on his dick to place it in her mouth. She moaned as her mouth maneuvered his dick in and out of her mouth. A few of her braids got in the way as her head bobbed to the beat of his moaning.

He grabbed her braids into a ponytail to assist her to take more of him in her mouth.

"Just like that," he said as she continued to give him head.

Greg watched in amazement at how her mouth moved. Her moaning was turning him on. He was sad that the Giants weren't winning. He wanted to put all of his dick in her mouth.

Damian wasted no time and whipped his dick out and watched as his beautiful girlfriend gave that sloppy toppy to his best friend. He was going to bust before halftime ended.

Laila was impressed by Tavon's dick.. It was not thick like Damian's dick but it was longer than Damian's. She had to use two hands to give Tavon a blowjob.

She watched Damian as he stroked himself to her motions. This was really turning her on. She made sure to work harder on Tavon's dick. At this point, she didn't care which guy fucked her after the game, she just knew she needed a dicking.

Tavon watched as she pulled his dick out of her mouth. She slid the slippery muscle in between her breasts and let him titty fuck her.

She did it for way longer than he thought she would. He was about to bust.

"Shit!" Tavon said between clenched teeth. He let his dick slide between her breasts into her mouth.

"That's right. Eat this dick whole, Laila."

All three of the guys didn't care what the sports analysts were saying on the halftime report. They were enthralled by Laila's skills.

She could taste his precum in her mouth, and she wasn't going to stop. Not even when Damian busted on himself.

She grinned evilly as he walked to the bathroom to clean himself.

"Can I come on your titties?" Tavon asked.

"Please," she begged, looking into his eyes.

"You have some sexy-ass eyes," he said, looking into her doe-like eyes.

He grabbed his dick and started stroking the sticky and wet phallus to get himself closer to his release.

He growled like an animal as he busted his load over her breasts.

"Give it all to me," she said as the hot liquid shot over that bikini top and her breasts. He stuffed the tip of his dick in her mouth, and she swallowed the remaining nut.

His body shook as she did that.

She smiled up at him as she released his tip from her mouth. He pulled his pants up and sat back down on the sofa spent.

Damian came back and helped Laila off her knees. They walked to the bathroom together to get her cleaned up.

Tavon looked at Greg and said, "What are we getting ourselves into? I can't believe I just did that."

"I never thought our best friend would let us smash. I've never wanted to smash her," Greg said. "When he told us about it yesterday, I didn't pay attention to what he was saying."

"Me either," Tavon said. "I have never thought about sexual encounters with her."

He got up from the chair and went to the other bathroom to clean himself.

When he came back to the living room, Laila was in a different bikini, but she winked at him before getting comfortable on the love seat.

Greg prayed that the Giants would win because he wanted to slide up in her. Her new bathing suit was a shimmering purple and silver bikini that had her breasts pronounced and covered her ass more than the last one.

Now that halftime was over, she went to sit in Damian's lap.

"Baby. I'm horny as hell," she said in his ear.

"I know, baby," he said. "But the guys got you covered. It was sexy as hell seeing you on your knees for Tav. I still can't believe you were up for this."

"Well, I be wearing you out so much. I needed fresh meat."

The two kissed.

For the next half of the game, the fellas kept her busy with their need for food and drinks.

Everyone was glued to the scene for the last three minutes into the game, the Patriots were still winning. However, the Giants weren't too far behind.

Laila and Damian started cleaning up the den and the kitchen.

But then they heard a commotion from the den.

"Overtime?" Greg said. "No way."

"This has been a tight game, bruh," Tavon said to him.

"I had money riding on this game with a coworker," he told Tavon.

"They might do their thing during overtime," Tavon told him. "Let's just watch the overtime."

"No. The hell we won't," Damian said, drying his

hands off and going into the den. "My girl is horny as fuck. She fucking one of y'all today."

He turned off the television and said, "I know it's a tie. But one of you is going to have sex with her. She has fucked me the last four days, and I finally recuperated this morning."

Greg and Tavon still can't believe Damian can't keep up with Laila's sex drive.

"What the hell we're supposed to do when there is a tie? Do rock, paper, scissors?" Greg asked.

"I'm not doing rock, paper, scissors for pussy," Tavon said. "I'm not doing a coin toss either. Let's ask her what she wants to do."

Laila walked into the den and said, "I was going to suggest that. My lust is in overdrive, and I need dick."

All three of them looked at her as she declared this.

"Since the game is tied. I believe it is only fair I fuck you both."

"Whoa there!" Damian said. "Are you up to that? I thought we decided on just one."

"I can handle it," she assured him.

"I mean it sounds like she has the energy for two," Greg said to Damian.

"The woman has spoken," Tavon said, staring at her.

She stared back and bit her bottom lip.

"But this wasn't in the plans," Damian said,

pulling her to the side. "I don't know if I can handle seeing both of them with you. I was only expecting one. It was easy seeing you give head, but both of them all over you, I'm not sure I can handle it."

"I know, baby, but I need this," she said, holding his hands. "If it gets too much for me, I'll stop. I promise. You don't have to be here for this either."

"Hell no," he said. "I'm going to be here."

"So this is a go?" she inquired.

Damian let out a shaky sigh and said, "Yes it is."

The two kissed, and he went to their bedroom to grab the box of condoms they'd purchased earlier that morning.

When he came back to the den, Tavon and Greg were walking Laila to the three-seater. The two men were fully naked. As she sat on the sofa, Tavon took her bikini bottom off of her. Greg released her breasts from the bikini top.

"Lay on your back sexy," Greg told her.

Greg grabbed a pillow, placed it on the floor, got on his knees, and started kissing her lips.

Damian watched as his girlfriend exchanged kisses with his best friend. Their lips worked well together as Greg kissed her softly to get her more comfortable.

Meanwhile, Tavon was more worried about her other set of lips. He got on the sofa in between her legs and lowered his head to give her head.

The feel of his lips peppering kisses on her pussy lips took her by surprise at first, but she smiled as she realized what Tavon was doing. Damian could hear her moans as she kissed Greg.

She pulled from the kiss and looked down at Tavon giving her head, and the sight was sexy.

Greg grabbed his dick, stroked it a few times, and put the tip in her mouth. Her lips spread wide to grab the mushroom-shaped dick. He watched in awe as she adjusted her body on the sofa to accommodate all of him. HIs dick was thick and shorter than Damian's, but she didn't care. His dick tasted good.

The gurgling coming from her mouth turned Tavon on. He pulled his head up to watch the show in front of him.

"You are so fucking pretty," Tavon told her.

"Just like that pretty girl," Greg told her as he slid himself in and out of her mouth.

"Yo, D!" Tavon yelled at Damian. "Pass me a condom."

Damian passed him one and watched to make sure he put it on correctly. He didn't need any mishaps.

Tavon placed his tip at Laila's entrance as he watched her slobber Greg down some more.

"You better take that dick like a pro," Greg said, warning her.

She used her hand to pat on her pussy. She pulled

Greg out of her mouth and said, "Come and get this pussy then, Tav."

Tavon entered her pussy, and her eyes closed, and she said, "Oh my God."

Tavon wasn't slow with his strokes either. He was stroking her insides like his life depended on it.

Damian couldn't lie. It was sexy as hell watching her take both of their dicks eloquently.

For the next seven minutes, he watched as his girlfriend took Tavon's strokes so well. She wasn't playing games while she sucked Greg's dick.

The two men constantly told the woman how beautiful she looked with dick in her mouth and in her pussy. They told her they wanted this moment to last forever.

She didn't complain as they aggressively kneaded her breasts or slapped her ass, she actually begged for more of it.

Damian's dick was getting hard watching them. His thoughts burst when he heard Tavon grunt out, "Fuck Laila! I'm coming."

She clenched her walls together to get him closer to his peak.

Tavon collapsed on her as he nutted in the condom. Greg told her to open her mouth wide, and he nutted in her mouth.

After both men came off their high, they asked her if she was okay.

"Do we need to stop?" Tavon asked.

Damian looked at his girlfriend for an answer. Her breathing was back to normal. Her braids were sticking to her skin. Her skin was glowing from the perspiration. Saliva was all over her chin.

"I'm fine," she assured all three men. "I have to wash my face," she said, getting off the sofa.

Damian followed her into their bathroom and helped her wash her face. He grabbed a scrunchie and helped her tie her braids into a high ponytail. He couldn't believe she still had the energy to go again.

It was alluring to see her stamina.

They walked back into the room. Tavon was on the loveseat by himself, resting. Greg was on the three-seater. His dick was in his hand and it was hard as a rock. She felt like it was calling her name.

"This time I want Damian to kiss me while I ride Greg's dick," Laila said before putting Greg in her mouth.

Damian was going to do more than kiss her. He was gonna fuck her after Greg did. He passed Greg a condom. Damian took his clothes off and sat on the three-seater while he watched Greg properly put the condom on. Laila climbed on Greg's lap, grabbed his condom-covered dick and inserted it in her.

She turned her face to Damian and he started kissing her as Greg slowly thrust himself in her.

Tavon was tired, but he watched for the next few minutes as she bounced her ass on Greg's dick. Damian even stood on the sofa to put his dick in Laila's mouth. Her ass bounced like a basketball as she rocked herself on Greg's dick.

All three men watched in awe as she came all over Greg's dick during her orgasm. Her pussy was juicier than Minute Maid. Greg's dick slipped out of her.

"I want you in my ass, Damian," she told her boyfriend. "Please," she begged.

Damian and Greg maneuvered themselves so that Greg was lying on his back.

She was still on top of Greg, but Damian could have access to her asshole. He didn't put on a condom; he just slipped his tip into her asshole. He eased the rest of him in her, and she cussed wildly.

It was a match made in heaven. She didn't have to do much work because with every stroke Greg gave her, it pushed her onto Damian's dick.

She and Damian had started doing anal a few months ago, and he had perfected his performance since.

Tavon watched as the two men worked her two tight holes and Greg came first. The house was full of the cacophony of her yelps and the two men's growls. She looked like she was horseback riding.

Damian held her ass cheeks like basketballs as he nutted in her asshole.

"Yes, baby!" she exclaimed. "Give me all that nut."

Damian pulled out of her slowly and loved seeing the white substance flow out of her hole.

He climbed off of her as he came back to his senses.

She felt empty back there. Thankfully, Greg was still in her.

Damian helped her off Greg.

Her legs felt wobbly as she stood up. She fell into Damian's arms.

This was the first time in a long time where Damian actually saw her look worn out. He held her in his arms as he saw Greg get off the sofa and walk to the bathroom.

"You were amazing, baby," Damian told her. "I didn't think you could handle it, baby girl."

"I can't stop smiling," she said. "I liked y'all taking turns on me."

Damian shook his head at his girlfriend's libido.

"I'm glad you enjoyed it," he told her before kissing her lips.

"Tav," Damian said. "While I go shower, can you run her a bath?"

Tavon obliged and helped her walk to the bathroom.

Ten minutes later, the guys were cleaned, dressed, and came back to the den. They turned on the television as they heard Laila singing from the bathtub.

"Who do you think won?" Greg asked.

"Who the fuck thinking about a game?" Tavon and Damian said in unison.

"I know I'm not," Tavon said. "Hell. We all hit touchdowns with Laila."

"You ain't lying," Damian said. "It was game time in that pussy."

The Male Prostitute
By Jade St. James

ASIA COULD NOT BELIEVE how beautiful the Black man that stood before her was. She knew his name was Shawn.

And Shawn was about to make her drool. His online picture did not display he was this fine.

The man was about five eleven. The five-foot-tall woman had to look up to see into his eyes.

His eyebrows were perfect. His button nose fit him perfectly. His eyes were hazel with thick eyelashes. Those lips were plump, and she wanted them between her legs.

"Shawn," she said to him. "You are on time and oh so fine."

Shawn licked his bottom lip and said, "Promptness is my middle name."

Asia escorted him in and as she took his jacket, she

looked at his butt. It wasn't too large or too small but the perfect ass. She could tell he worked out.

"Let's head to the living room," she told him.

He followed her into the living room. The Black woman was beautiful. She was thicker than what he was used to. Her backside was protruding in her dress. It was a mustard lace dress that barely came to her knees. She was wearing fishnet stockings and cheetah heels.

After admiring the well-put-together woman, Shawn saw a white man comfortable on one of the sofas. The man had a slight tan to him, brown hair on his head, and he was only in a wifebeater and basketball shorts.

"That's Kevin—my husband," Asia said to Shawn. "He's not a real man, and he needs to see how a queen like me deserves to be fucked."

"Understood," Shawn said.

Shawn wasn't shocked. He'd only been in the sex business for a year and he'd already had five women who had cuckolds for husbands. Their husbands enjoyed watching Shawn take their wives to their peak.

Shawn and Asia settled on the other sofa. He blocked Kevin out of his mind and focused on Asia.

Asia's face did not have a blemish. Her skin was smoother than peanut butter. Her eyelashes were wispy. Her black hair had bouncy romance curls.

Shawn usually disliked when women wore lip gloss before sex, but her chocolate brown lip gloss was the icing on the cake.

"I see you dressed for the weather and not the occasion," she told him.

Shawn looked down at his ensemble and stated, "The weather is too cold for me to be in my boxers and shirtless, ma'am."

She gave a coy smile.

Asia looked at his attire—a chocolate brown sweater was a little loose on his tight body. His cock print was visible in his white dress pants.

"Here's how today will work," she said. "I have you for one hour. I prefer sex on the kitchen table and on the sofa. Subtle kisses get me going. No French kisses. My hot spots are my neck and my knees."

Shawn laughed.

"Your knees? You're that sensitive?"

"It's a blessing and a curse," she stated.

Kevin laughed at his wife from the other chair.

"And don't forget we have Kevin as a guest."

Asia crawled over to Shawn and sat on his lap.

"Do you have any notes for me?" she asked him.

"Not at all," he said. "I'm just in awe that a woman as beautiful as you needs my services."

"I purchased your services as a want, not a need," she said, pulling his chin closer to her lips.

Shawn looked at her lips. Then in her eyes. Back at her lips. He couldn't resist her lips.

She wrapped her arm around his shoulder for balance and kissed back.

It wasn't until then that she noticed he had a light cologne scent on him. It was enticing.

He adjusted their position so she could feel his cock wanting to free itself. Shawn started to get aggressive with his kisses.

She pulled back and looked into his eyes and spoke sternly. "I said subtle kisses."

"I'm sorry, Asia," he said, softening the kiss.

This was going to be an interesting client. Most of his clients were female. Ninety percent of the time, they preferred aggressive kisses.

He was curious why in her online notes, she'd notated wanting to be fucked hard but treated softly.

Shawn had no idea why this woman had purchased his services, but he hoped they both could enjoy it.

Asia was mesmerized by Shawn's kisses. She was so glad they'd found him online to make Kevin's fantasy a reality.

Her husband had always wanted to see Asia get fucked by a Black man. It was their ten-year wedding anniversary, and he felt it was the perfect time to do it.

Asia was not used to kissing a stranger, but Shawn

was making her feel comfortable. His large hands rubbed over her back as she kissed his chin.

Her body was warm all over, and she couldn't stop smiling.

"My neck please," she told him.

His supple lips navigated their way to the right side of her neck, where he used his tongue and teeth to mark her up. He hoped it was getting her wet because he was ready to enter her pussy, and he didn't want to hurt her.

Shawn heard her giggle and squeal from his mouth action and was glad she was giving him the cues he needed. If she wanted to be treated like a queen, he would do just that. His lips moved to the left side of her neck, and she was really squealing now.

Kevin cleared his throat. While it was nice to see his wife enjoy herself, it was hard to take that it was with another man. A man she chose, that was a little younger than her and Kevin, and she was responding so well to this male prostitute.

Asia pulled from the kiss and said, "We don't care, Kevin. Don't be mad that somebody is taking your place today. You asked for this."

Shawn had to smile at her assertive remark before he went back to foreplay.

His lips sprinkled kisses from her neck crevice to

her ear. His voice was a little huskier as he said, "Tell me what you want. Be my boss. I'll be inferior."

Asia couldn't think of what to say.

"It's okay," he said. "I'm patient."

He went back to kissing her.

Asia noticed her nipples were starting to tingle, and she felt a wanting in her pussy. To alleviate that feeling, she started grinding on the protruding spot in his pants. She knew he could feel the motions because he matched her movements.

"I'm serious," he said back in her ear. "Use me."

"I'm hot," she told him in between breaths.

"Hold your curls." He made reference to her hair as he carefully found the bottom of her dress. The dress was bunched up between them, but he carefully pulled it over her head.

Asia didn't care if her hair was out of place; she was relieved to feel the cool air on her skin.

Her burgundy bralette could barely hold her size F breasts. It was a sight that Shawn liked to see.

While she reciprocated and removed his sweater, all Shawn could think was, *She doesn't know it, but I'm fixing to make her a buffet.*

He was going to sample each portion of her body he could.

Shawn's hand pushed her bralette down to expose her heavy breasts. He still had her balanced on his lap, but he kissed her lips while he twisted her nipple. No nipple was left behind as he used the next few minutes to twist and suck the sensitive pieces of flesh.

This usually didn't turn her on, but today it did. Shawn's foreplay made her want him more.

"Just like that," she said as she watched him do this. "Kevin, take notes. I disliked it before, but I now like my nipples being sucked."

Shawn finished working on her nipples by kissing her on the lips. He moved her to the side of him, and she noticed he was about to remove his pants.

"I got you, sweetheart," she said, pulling his pants down. His dick sprang out—already hard.

He typically had women give him head to get him hard. But foreplay had him harder than a Jolly Rancher today. He didn't need head. He stroked himself a few times to see what she would do.

It had been over twelve years since she had last been with a man other than Kevin. The size of that dick made her nervous.

"Don't be scared," Shawn said to her. "My dick doesn't bite."

Asia tucked her curls behind her ears and said, "I don't know about that, baby. That thing looks like it can do damage."

"It'll do whatever you want it to do," he told her.

The veins were there and made her want to drool. She couldn't wait to feel his cock in her hand.

"Damn, Kevin," she said to her husband as she grabbed Shawn's dick. "This might be too much dick for me. I might not come back to your tiny-ass dick after this."

Kevin looked at his basketball shorts. He didn't even have a print on display.

"You can't handle all that Black cock," Kevin said. "I know you can't."

Shawn didn't care about this conversation. Asia had already started stroking his cock.

"Fuck it," she whispered to herself. She was going to go through with it. She needed her money's worth.

She let her tongue swirl around his tip and on the two veins that caught her attention. Her lips grazed the base of his penis. Then her lips engulfed the tip and the first inch of him. Shawn's eyes closed tightly as he enjoyed the feeling of being in her mouth. He watched as her mouth and hand utilized teamwork to get him slippery.

He smacked her ass while he watched her work.

The woman's hand stroked him while the other hand held his balls before she gently put them in her mouth.

"Shit!" Kevin exclaimed.

She finished with his balls and went back to having his dick in her mouth.

A few moments ago, Asia had looked scared of the dick, but now she was swallowing it.

"Yeah. Keep that up," Shawn said to her as he pumped himself in her mouth. She placed her hand on his six-pack for balance and to slow him down.

It didn't slow him down, though. He placed his hand on the back of her neck to keep her there. She was deepthroating perfectly. He wanted to come in her mouth so badly, but he wasn't one to come quickly.

Kevin watched as his wife handled the strange man's cock in her mouth. They had a chemistry going, and he wasn't mad at it. He licked his lips at every gag noise his wife made and loved how Shawn talked her through how to pleasure him.

Kevin felt that if this was how beautiful foreplay was, he could only imagine the masterpiece the two would make on the sofa and the kitchen table.

Shawn pulled her off his cock and kissed her. He was so hungry for her lips, but he remembered subtle kisses were the key to her responding well to him. He needed to get her out of her underwear. He wanted to pleasure her while she had the fishnets on.

He knew how to multitask and kiss her while moving her underwear to the side. When he fingered her, he was full of joy while feeling how wet she was.

He felt like his fingers were playing with a small glass of water.

Her juices were making loud sloshing noises, and he wanted to taste her. His kisses trailed from her lips to her breasts, to her muffin top, and down to her clit. He let his lips suck on the sensitive bulb as he fingered her.

Then his tongue plunged into her pussy, and she started cussing. Her taste was so unique, and he lapped up her juices like a dog lapped water.

She was beyond wet for him, and he stroked his cock while he feasted on her pussy.

He removed himself from her and said, "I want you on top."

Shawn lay on his back and pulled her on top of him. She grabbed his cock to sit on it.

"You got me fucked up," Kevin said from the sofa. "Put on a fucking condom."

Shawn and Asia had gotten tested and shared the results with each other. They both had healthy results. Asia didn't mind him going raw.

"No. Little Peter," she said to her husband.

Kevin waved her off and said, "Whatever."

She centered Shawn's tip at her entrance. She bounced on the head a little bit to prepare herself.

"You got this, Asia," Shawn said from beneath her. "Just let it slide in."

The Black woman let the tip slide in, and they both groaned in pleasure. Her pussy felt full.

"I want more of your cock," she said to him.

"I'm not going to stop you," he said, putting his hands on her hips.

She slid down some more on him, and he started pumping his hips up to start a flow for them.

His pumps weren't slow but intermediate, and she wasn't complaining.

It created good friction for both of them.

Asia couldn't take all of him. She knew there were about two inches she was not even using. She didn't want to overthink, so she wasted no time bouncing on Shawn.

Her hands used the sofa as leverage as she rode him like a trained equestrian. His cock was like a black stallion. He would never let her fall off. Her curls framed her face and bounced with her as she rode Shawn.

"You were nervous for no fucking reason," he whispered to her. "You taking my dick like a professional."

She and Kevin didn't talk much during sex, but this was a nice change.

Shawn kissed her as she rode him.

They did that for a few minutes until Shawn carefully got them off the sofa and started fucking her while he stood up. His hands gripped her ass, and he planted his feet as her legs wrapped around his waist and he bounced her on his cock.

Asia was moaning like crazy, and Kevin pulled his dick out of his pants. He watched as his wife took Shawn so well. Their sex noises were an intricate mix that was the background he needed to bust.

His hand movements were slow as he looked on. He couldn't believe this prostitute was fucking his wife in the air.

He was sure her pussy was stretched wide for Shawn.

Shawn was kissing Asia as he slammed her down on his dick.

Her ass was clapping like a stadium of fans, and he loved it.

Then he laid her back on the sofa. He got on the sofa on his knees and started fucking her hard. She tried to put her hand on his abdomen to slow him down, but he just held her hand tight as he rocked her into ecstasy. She used her free hand to grip her curls.

"Shawn. I feel like a geyser."

"Good," he said.

Asia squirted on him for a few seconds. He pulled out and used the liquid as lubrication and put himself back in her.

He started rubbing on her clit as he stroked her.

"Kevin don't ever fuck me like this," she said between her panting.

"Mess around, I'll have you walking with a limp," Shawn said.

"Uh-huh," she told him. They locked eye contact. "Don't stop. I want a limp."

That was all he needed to hear to work harder to please her. He knew she needed a few more strokes.

It did the trick.

She squirted again, and he smiled widely.

Shawn started eating her out, and she couldn't stop cussing. She pushed his head away because she couldn't take it. His hands kneaded her breasts as she did so.

Kevin couldn't believe it. It had been months since she'd squirted with him.

Shawn came up for air and asked her to ride again.

The ball was in her court, and she was doing any type of rhythm to come on him.

She wrapped her arms around his neck as they worked in collaboration to hit the finish line.

"Don't hold it in," he told her.

Her strokes stopped as she collapsed on his chest, calling his name. He continued to pump in her because he was close.

He pulled out and came on her ass.

"Oh yes!" she exclaimed. "Give it all to me."

Shawn was tired.

"My God!" he said, kissing all over her face. "Exceptional."

She didn't know why, but she felt accomplished. And she felt like a new person.

Asia did feel a little sore in between her legs. But she didn't complain.

They heard whimpering and panting and saw Kevin masturbating.

"Shawn, can you eat her out again while I watch?" he said. Kevin turned his attention to his wife and said, "I'm not going to last long."

Shawn and Asia shrugged and did as they were told. Kevin walked over to Asia and looked at her love faces as Shawn ate her pussy nice and slowly.

"I'm going to come," Kevin said, looking at his wife as she twisted her nipples and enjoyed Shawn tasting her.

He advised Shawn to move. Shawn did what he was told and walked into the kitchen. He hoped a downstairs bathroom was there.

Kevin spilled his seed on Asia's tits. And she said, "Keep coming, baby. Put that hot cum on me."

She looked like a Toaster Strudel, and it turned him on.

"I fucking love you!" Kevin said as he bent down to kiss her. The two went upstairs to clean themselves.

Asia had about 30 more minutes with Shawn. And she was glad. She didn't want him to leave yet.

She desired another round with him.

Shawn was glad he found the downstairs bathroom. There weren't many washcloths in there, but he was able to find one. He used hot water and soap to clean himself up.

While doing that, all he could think about was how it was an amazing experience with Asia. He wasn't sure what she was nervous for; she'd handled him well. Her moans weren't ugly and annoying, but more sensual in nature.

Her pussy was like a snug glove on his cock, and he didn't mind at all.

Typically, he wore a condom with clients. But having raw, consensual sex with her was a marvelous feeling. A world that was smooth, warm, and felt like a sweet dream. They had a spark together.

Shawn was glad he had more time with her because he wasn't ready to leave. He wanted to bury his cock in her pussy until she begged for rest.

When he walked out of the bathroom naked, he saw Kevin and a naked Asia removing items off their kitchen table. He couldn't keep his eyes off her. He noticed some fruit on the table and a small vibrator.

Kevin looked a little more relaxed than thirty minutes ago. Maybe this was what he needed to see.

"You took that cock so well," Kevin told Asia.

"His cock is on a different level, baby," she said to Kevin. "I want him back in me."

Shawn sat on the kitchen table. It was a bit cold against his skin, but he thugged through it. She walked in between his legs and didn't break contact.

Kevin rinsed off the fruit for the couple and had a small container of warm chocolate placed on the table with it.

Afterward, he sat in one of the table chairs to watch the two get to work.

Asia started kissing Shawn on his lips. He ignited a fire in her, and she started tugging on his bottom lip roughly.

Shawn pulled back and said, "Subtle kisses. Remember?"

Asia couldn't help but laugh. He was using her words on her. She was hungry for him.

She grabbed a strawberry and dipped it into the chocolate. She was careful not to drop the warm liquid on them. She watched his plump lips take ninety percent of the strawberry in.

She knew in a few moments she would be the "strawberry." She watched as he chewed the sweet fruit so slowly.

He grabbed a strawberry and swirled it into the

warm chocolate. He fed her the strawberry, and her lips looked so good around it.

Just like her lips around his cock.

Shawn kissed her between the bites of strawberries.

She tried to feed him another.

"This is sexy as hell," he told her. "But I didn't come here to eat fruit."

"Last one, I promise," she said feeding him another.

She went to go wash her hands.

Asia walked right back between his legs and interlocked their lips. Their lips were like magnets as she softly kissed him. She gave a slight tug on his bottom lip, which still had a sweet chocolate taste.

Her warm hands slid down each ridge on his six-pack as she kissed him. She used one hand to travel to his cock, never breaking the kiss.

She stroked him. He loved how she was firm and slow with her hands.

It wasn't taking him long to get hard, and she loved it.

"I want you in my mouth, but I didn't think this through. I don't want the food to fuck up your cock or my pH."

"Y'all don't have a lubricant in the house we could use?" he asked between kisses.

Kevin got up and said, "I got y'all."

"Go do that small cock," she said to her husband.

When he came back, he passed Asia the lubricant. She squirted some in her hand and coated Shawn's dick with it.

His cock looked so shiny, she was ready to have him in her. She smeared a bit on her pussy lips.

"Let me fuck you again," he said, getting off the table. "Arch your back and let me do it from behind."

Asia assumed the position and placed her hands on the kitchen table as she bent over.

Shawn grabbed his cock and slid into Asia effortlessly.

"Shit," he hissed out. He didn't know what it was about this woman, but he felt like she was the lock and he was the key.

"On God, your pussy feels like it's meant for me," he said.

Kevin would have probably rolled his eyes at something like this, but he liked how the couple looked.

They really did move melodically. There was a different type of passion in how they moved harmoniously.

Their bodies were starting to sweat, Asia had the sexiest sounds flowing from her mouth, and their movements looked like a uniformed machine.

The way Shawn's hand rested perfectly in the arch on Asia's lower back helped their movements. His other hand gripped her ass cheek. It was soft in his hand, and he couldn't help but squeeze it.

Asia felt like his cock was the key to a new awakening for her. Shawn was opening her up to something different. Her pussy had a grasp that would soon take his soul. Their bond was fresh and new. Each stroke she had with him deepened the link they had with each other. Shawn knew they were two separate people, unifying as one.

A unity that was harmonious in nature for today only. They had solidarity with the ultimate goal of satisfying Asia and Kevin. Shawn loved that he had the key to enhancing her sexual experience that would be locked in her mind forever.

"Harder please," she asked him as she spread her ass cheeks wider.

It helped Shawn go deeper into her lock. His motions were forceful, but they gave her the friction she needed. The table rocked beneath them.

"That's right, queen," he said as he noticed she clenched herself around his cock.

Her hands were tired, and she placed them back on the table for support.

"Come here, queen," he said, placing his hand on her muffin top. Shawn pulled her back into his chest and kissed her.

Their interconnection was a beautiful sight for

Kevin to see. Shawn had large hands and used them to massage Asia's breasts during the kiss.

He pushed her back into her bent position.

"See, Kevin!" Asia said. "His cock is long enough to fuck me from the back and kiss me. You can't do that with that small cock."

Kevin didn't care what she said. His cock was in his hand as he enjoyed the show.

Shawn maintained his focus on Asia, and she said, "I got it from here."

Shawn held his hands on his hips as Asia threw her ass back on him. She held on to the bowl of chocolate for balance.

Every time she threw it on him, they both had to let it be known how good it felt.

"You like me fucking you?" he asked as her ass cheeks clapped. Her ass clapped like a round of applause in the kitchen.

"Yes Shawn!" she exclaimed. "Don't stop."

He grabbed her hands and placed them behind her on her arch as he stroked in her harder and faster. The kitchen table rocked beneath them.

She squirted on the floor and screamed loudly.

Shawn loved it. Her juices pushed him out of her, so he pulled out and stroked himself.

He saw the precum on his tip and told her to turn over.

Now on her back, the cold table cooled down her skin. Her mouth had the perfect o-shape, and her eyes rolled to the back of her head when he entered her missionary style.

"I'm finna come in you," he told her in between kisses.

"Please," she begged.

It didn't take long for to him do it.

An animalistic growl escaped his lips as he hit his peak. Asia thought it felt so good to feel his warm seed spill inside her.

The pair kissed each other as they heard Kevin panting.

Shawn took this as his cue to move. He pulled out of her and walked to the bathroom. As he entered the bathroom, he heard Kevin howl.

Asia said, "That's right, baby. Keep coming on my breasts, Kevin."

Shawn shook his head. Being a male prostitute was an interesting profession.

Let's Be Honest
By Kendra K.

"You need to get your ass out of the house," Ray told his best friend, Kat.

"I'm not in the mood," she said.

"Just because you had a breakup doesn't mean it's the end of the world," the dark-skinned man said, running his hand through his starter locs.

"This is still a fresh breakup, Ray," she said, glaring at him. "I've had two boyfriends and a situationship in the last four years."

"I know this," he said, glaring back at her. "But I need you to leave the apartment."

The two were having their stare-down in her studio apartment. She had just had a breakup two weeks before. She'd been going to work as needed and light grocery shopping, but that was it.

"Let me help you get your mind off things," he

asked, stepping into her small closet to find her an outfit.

"It's noon. I don't want to go anywhere."

"We're going to get drinks," he said while finding two outfits. "Now go get dressed, bitch," he said.

He walked to her bathroom and turned the shower on.

The light-skinned girl grudgingly got up and grabbed a shower cap before she walked into her bathroom.

Ray walked to her small kitchen table and said, "Maybe you'll thank me later."

When she came out thirty minutes later, she had on a cheetah bra with matching cheetah underwear. Her blond and black hair was in a tight afro puff on top of her head.

"All right," she said, putting studs in her ears. "What outfits have you found for me?"

"The best outfits to bitch about men in," he said. "A pair of jeans and this shirt or this purple cami with your plaid black skirt."

Kat rolled her eyes. "Ray, where are we going?"

"The best gay bar in the city."

"Why do you want to bitch about men with me anyway?" she inquired. "You're in a healthy relationship with your man," she pointed out.

"I'm here for moral support," he said, passing her the jeans and shirt combo.

"Whatever," the slender woman huffed, putting on the clothes.

She looked in her full-length mirror and noticed she was losing weight. Her breasts were still full and perky. Her ass still had the nice cup to it. But she was losing weight in the abdomen area.

Maybe this breakup was helpful after all.

Kat put on lip gloss but no other makeup, and put on a fresh pair of boots to head to the bar.

She grabbed a jacket, her purse, and her keys.

In Ray's car, they listened to great breakup songs, "Leave (Get Out)," "Irreplaceable," and "Thank U Next."

When they arrived at the bar, it already had a decent crowd. There were about two dozen people in there either eating or drinking. The men and women inside this bar were beautiful.

They all seemed to be having a great time.

"I'm not going to lie," she said as they sat on a bar chair. "It feels good to see other people than my coworkers."

"You're welcome," Ray said.

Kat playfully nudged him.

She ordered three martinis for herself while Ray ordered Disarono and raspberry juice.

"Ray. Let me tell you how I really have been feeling," she said as they waited on their drinks.

"I want to open up my dating pool," she said.

"How so?" Ray asked.

"My last few boyfriends have been the same. But I also know I met them in similar circles. I want to go into dating circles I've never been in before. I've dealt with a man who was on the road all the time for work. I've been with a man who was the perfect provider, but he didn't have emotions. I felt like I couldn't show my emotions around him."

"You know how us men are," Ray said. "Especially us Black men."

"I know," she said as she grabbed her first two martinis from the bartender.

Ray told the bartender to leave the tab open as he received his drink.

"I've dated outside my race before," she said. "But I need to find a man who likes to occasionally be by himself but still loves to be around me. I want to find a man who is not just the provider but also healthily shows his emotions."

"I think that man is out there for you," Ray said. "But he may not be in your dating pool yet."

"How you mean?" she asked her best friend.

"You and I met three years ago. Only because I moved to this town. What if the man you're looking for hasn't moved here yet? Or what if he does live here, but you two haven't been in the same circles yet?"

"I think you're on to something there," she said. "It's timing. He and I haven't met yet."

"Exactly," Ray said taking a sip of his drink. "Unless you're ready to date a woman," he joked.

"I'm a hot mess," she said. "No woman would want me."

Ray started laughing. "Yes. You are."

The two continued laughing and joking.

Kat finished her two martinis and was ready for her third.

"I'm starting to get tipsy," she said. "This is my last one."

"Understood," he said. "You see I've been babysitting my drink. I have to drive us home."

The two then started a conversation about Ray's mishaps with dating Black men. It was crazy interesting for both of them that they had similar dating problems.

Except the man Ray was with now was a higher tier of men than Ray had dated before.

"I just want to put his attributes in a bottle and sell it to folks," Kat joked. "We need more men like him out here."

"Amen," Ray said.

"Here you go ma'am," the bartender said while handing Kat a martini.

"I haven't ordered a drink in about 15 minutes," Kat said.

"That lovely lady ordered this for you." The bartender gave a head nod to a woman about three tables from the bar.

"She's cute," Ray and Kat said to each other.

The woman was svelte, caramel skin tone, and her hair looked silkier than the blue dress she had on. It was the perfect dress for a day party. Her fedora hat was the icing to her outfit.

She waved and winked at Kat.

Kat gave a "thank you" nod from her seat.

She returned her attention back to Ray, and he said, "Go invite her over here."

"You think I should?" she asked.

"Yes."

"But I'm not into women," she said to her best friend.

"It doesn't matter. She could be a future comrade. She could lead you into a new dating pool."

Kat thought about what her best friend was saying. And thought, *Why not?*

"I'll be right back," she told Ray.

She got off the bar stool and smoothed down

possible wrinkles on her outfit. She grabbed her drink and walked over to the cute woman's table.

The woman's eyes followed Kat with every step she took.

Kat was starting to blush a bit under her gaze.

"May I have a seat with you?" she asked the woman with thick eyelashes.

"Absolutely, darling," the woman said in a sultry voice.

"I'm Kat. Thank you again for the drink."

"Kat. I'm Willow."

"Willow. Nice to meet you," she said, taking a sip of the fruity drink. "I'm over there discussing how annoyed I am with dating men."

"They really know how to get under our skin, don't they?"

"Yes," Kat chuckled.

Willow tucked her hair behind her ear and said, "Who's the handsome gentleman?"

"My best friend, Ray," she said. "He's bitching about men with me. Even though he has a great boyfriend."

"Oh. So you're not together?" Willow asked, taking a sip of her own drink.

"Not at all," Kat giggled.

"Good," Willow said. "I don't want to flirt with a woman that is spoken for."

Kat's face was getting warm from embarrassment again. She started playing with the salt shaker on the table.

"Cat's got your tongue, huh, Kat? Pun intended."

The two laughed.

"The cat does," she said, playing with the earring in her ear.

"Well, tell me about yourself. Let's loosen up a bit."

For the next twenty minutes, the two ladies chatted about themselves. There was a spark between them, and Ray didn't want to intrude.

"I'm not going to lie," Willow said. "I'm trying to take you home with me."

"Me?"

"We're already vibing," she said. "You are as fine as wine, and I have to have a taste of you."

Kat gave a coy smile.

"Taste me?"

"Yes, sweetheart," Willow said.

Kat didn't know how Ray did it. But he came just in time.

"Hey, ladies. I hate to interrupt, but we have to get home," he said to Willow.

"That's right! You're my ride home. Let's go, bestie," Kat said, getting out of her seat.

"I was just telling Kat I think you two should come by my place," Willow said. "I don't live far."

"Let's give it a shot," Ray said.

Willow gave a charmed smile at Kat's bewildered face.

"What's your number? I'll give you my address in case you get lost."

Willow and Kat exchanged numbers.

Ray and Kat hopped in Ray's car and followed Willow.

"So are you going to fuck her?" Ray asked once they were in the car.

"Ray!" she said. "I can't. I don't even know her."

"She seems like a sweet woman," Ray told her.

"Ray. She could be a murderer."

"The way she looks . . . she looks like she wants to murder your pussy."

Kat covered her face with her hands as Ray cackled.

"I'm leaving you with her," he said.

"I'm not ready," she said.

"Maybe you are. We'll just feel the vibes while we're there."

They pulled up to one of the nicer apartment buildings in the city. Ray parked in the visitor's parking.

"You can handle this," he said. "I'll leave you two alone, but I'll be here in the parking lot."

The best friends followed Willow inside the apartment building. Her apartment had a neosoul aesthetic. There were posters of Jill Scott, Musiq Soul Child, Floetry, and Maxwell. The woman turned on a Spotify playlist full of Sza and Ari Lennox songs.

The paintings inside were magnificent.

"You did these yourself?" Kat asked in amazement.

"I wish I could say I did. There's an artist at the local flea market. Every two weeks she has new paintings to sell. I buy from her and her brother often. He does various art forms too," Willow said, pointing out pottery pieces in her apartment.

"You all need water or snacks?" she asked.

"Cute and hospitable," Ray said. "Water please."

"I aim to please," Willow said, winking at Kat.

Kat couldn't stop blushing. The woman only said simple things to her, but she was still enamored.

All she could wonder was what she was getting herself into.

Willow passed Ray and Kat miniature water bottles. Kat took a sip instantly. She needed to cool down.

Willow started the conversation, and Kat felt like she was falling into a spell with each word she said. Kat was listening, but she paid attention to Willow's mouth. She couldn't believe she was thinking this, but Willow had a pretty mouth.

Her smile shone bright like a diamond, her lips looked like they knew how to envelop a clit, and her tongue looked heavy—in a good way.

Maybe she should take Ray's advice.

Kat took her mind out of the gutter and focused on the conversation.

It wasn't long before she was comfortable. Ray could look at her body language and tell he wasn't needed.

"All right, ladies," he said. "I'll see you later."

When he made it downstairs, he made sure to text his best friend that he was in the car. Ready to ride or die for her.

She texted him she was thankful for him.

Kat decided to make the first move.

"I've never kissed a woman before," she said. "But I want to kiss you."

"I see you had a change of heart," Willow said in her sultry voice.

"Oh yes," Kat said. "I see there is an attraction between us. I can't deny it. And I'm pretty sure you want to murder my pussy."

Willow busted out laughing. "I don't want to murder it. But I definitely want it to purr for me."

Willow removed her hat and moved it to the other side of her sofa. She smoothed her hair down and tucked it behind her ear before leaning in for a kiss.

In Kat's mind, she was frozen in a moment of time with Willow. There was a beautiful energy between the two of them. When their lips connected, Kat felt a sense of peace wash over her. The anticipation was over. It was as if the kiss was a soothing, nourishing feeling.

Willow pulled away, but Kat pulled her back in. The moment was gentle, carefree, and charming. It was like taking cookies out of the cookie jar. With each kiss, Kat wanted more.

Willow pulled back and asked, "Are you okay?"

"I'm perfectly fine," Kat said, looking into Willow's eyes. "You lead. I'll follow."

Effortlessly, Willow helped Kat get comfortable on the sofa. Kat was on her back while Willow made her way to Kat's face. The two kissed each other to the point where their tongues were fighting for dominance to explore each other's mouths.

Willow's lips could not stop veering to kiss Kat's cheeks. She nibbled on Kat's chin, always returning to her velvety lips.

The loud kissing noises bounced off the walls of the apartment.

"Your lips are so fucking juicy," Kat told Willow.

"Likewise," Willow said, palming Kat's breasts.

She wanted to motorboat the woman beneath her but decided not to.

"Undress me," she told Kat.

Kat unzipped the beauty's dress. Willow got off the sofa and shimmied her way out of it. Willow was wearing a white bra and panty set. A look so pure for the lustful moment.

Kat stood up and was ready to undress, but Willow had other ideas.

"I'll undress you," she said.

Willow took her time to undress Kat. She gave her kisses on the lips after removing her shirt.

Her lips kissed the top of her breasts. And she left a hickey on the sensitive skin. Her lips traveled to Kat's stomach, and she felt butterflies all over.

Willow unbuttoned Kat's jeans and kissed her thick thighs.

Kat wondered if Willow could feel the shivers going down her body.

"We have to stop," she said.

"Stop?" Willow asked, helping Kat out of her jeans.

She stood up and looked into Kat's eyes.

"I love men," Kat said. "I'm strictly dickly."

"Your actions tell me you're interested in this," Willow stated.

"I'm sure. I don't want to lead you on. I'm not gay."

"So I'll stop then," Willow said.

"But it feels so good."

"Let me please you," Willow said. "I'm going to give you the best head of your life, and then you can tell me if you're gay or at least gay for Willow."

"You'd better make it remarkable," Kat told Willow.

Willow grinned wickedly.

"I got you," she said, removing Kat's matching cheetah set.

She cupped both breasts in her hands and ran her tongue over each nipple. They looked like big chocolate chips.

Willow gently squeezed as she put one nipple in her mouth.

Kat let out a soft whine. She looked down to see how sexy Willow looked with that mouth on her nipple.

She moaned louder when Willow moved her mouth to Kat's other nipple.

"Fuck! You're making me wet," Kat said. Her hands moved to Kat's ass to explore.

"Damn. You got a body," Willow told her. "I want to feel on your ass all day."

"Keep touching me like this. It might happen."

For the next five minutes, Willow pleasured Kat while Kat lay on the sofa. She explored every inch of Kat's body with her fingers and mouth. Kat's body quivered with each passing minute. Her pussy felt nice and stretched when Willow hooked two fingers in her.

"Fuck. Don't stop," she said while rocking herself on Willow's fingers.

The gushiness of her pussy enhanced the moment.

"That's right, cutie. Get that shit."

Kat didn't come, but she squirted from Willow's actions.

Willow slowly pulled her fingers out of Kat and tasted them.

"Come and see how you taste," she told Kat.

The two kissed until the main event happened.

Willow positioned her face between Kat's legs and kissed Kat's clit and the pussy folds. Willow's tongue zig-zagged between the sensitive bulb and the folds.

Kat had only had one boyfriend ever eat her out. He was good at it, but Willow might be better.

Willow's tongue was heavy as it continued to do patterns on the pussy lips. Then she delved her tongue in there.

"My God," Kat blurted out.

Her tongue worked like a dick doing different angles inside of Kat. Kat looked down to watch the beauty pleasure her. It was a beautiful view, and it helped her better react to Willow more.

"Devour me," she told Willow.

When Kat least expected it, Willow sucked Kat's

clit. Her soul was about to be snatched. Willow continued to assault the bulb that sent Kat's nerves all over the place. Kat was starting to squeal in the apartment, and Willow loved it.

She started fingering the beauty as she sucked on the clit. Kat was writhing and holding on to pillows for balance. She was about to come and didn't know how to articulate it.

Willow's free hand roamed over Kat's body, and Kat loved it.

Then Willow said, "Can you get on all fours, sweetie? I want that fat ass in my face."

Kat did as she was told. While on all fours, Willow ate Kat's pussy from the back.

"Just like that," Kat said, finding a rhythm and throwing her ass back on Willow's tongue.

"I don't want you to stop," she said.

Willow took this as motivation and made her lips vibrate on Kat's pussy's lips. She rubbed on the voluminous ass cheeks as she did so.

"I'm coming," Kat said. "Please keep going."

Willow continued to work her magic as a human vibrator. Kat shrieked and felt butterflies in her stomach. Her breathing was coming faster. Willow did not let up on the pleasure. Kat clenched her pussy lips together to reach her climax faster.

Then the butterfly flutters left her stomach and spread all over her body.

"I just came on you," she drowsily said repeatedly.

Willow continued to feast on the woman's sensitive flesh. Kat's body quivered with each lick.

"I'm gay for Willow," Kat called out. "I'm gay for Willow."

Willow slowly removed her tongue from Kat and said, "That's what I like to hear."

Hot Ron
By Willa Porter

"Pop! I'm here," Erika yelled when she walked into her father-in-law's house.

"We're in the kitchen," he yelled back.

The twenty-eight-year-old walked to the kitchen. And of course, her father-in-law, Ron, and her son, Ron III, were about to eat dinner. Her son was only one, but a small portion of food was in front of him.

He was so stinking cute!

"How was your day?" the man asked, digging into his plate of food.

"Tiresome. I kind of thought this death stuff would be over with."

"Agreed."

Erika's husband, Ron Jr. had died from cancer six months ago. She couldn't believe she still had to communicate with xx and the insurance companies for certain stuff related to assets she and her husband had.

"I feel you go through more hoops now than I did when my wife died," Ron said.

Ron's wife Olivia had died when Ron Jr. was 20.

"I probably do, Pop," she said.

"Are you ready for next week?" Ron asked to change the topic.

"I'm nervous and excited," she said to the man. "It'll be early morning."

Erika had been in nursing school when Ron Jr. had gotten sick a year ago. She'd had to quit to tend to her husband. She felt she was ready to go back to school.

"Well, I'm here to support you. I know your folks will too," the fifty-year-old man said.

"Thanks," she said. "Are you still able to take him to daycare for me next week?"

"Absolutely!" he said. "I'll pick him up some evenings if I don't open the bar."

Ron owned a local bar in the area. He usually didn't open the bar until 4 p.m., but he had an excellent manager that stepped up to the plate for the business.

The small family unit finished dinner and said goodnight so Erika and the baby could go home.

The man didn't want them to leave, but he knew

he couldn't be in their face all the time. He got comfortable and ready for bed.

The days twirled into nights. Monday rolled around quickly, and Ron took his grandson to daycare.

All the teachers were excited to see the two. Staff knew Ron Jr.'s death had taken a toll on everyone.

Ron the Third, whom they also called R3, had only started coming back to daycare about a month ago.

"How have you been?" the daycare director asked Ron.

"We're holding up. You know we still miss him," Ron said.

"I bet you all do. We miss seeing his bright smile. You're the best grandad in town. You're always focusing on him and Erika. You make sure you make time for yourself."

"I will," he said.

"I want to introduce you to our two newest teachers. They started while your grandson was out. This is Vanessa, and this is Tracy. R3 is in Tracy's class."

Vanessa was a young woman. Tracy was a man. They didn't look a day over 21.

"Nice meeting you both," he said to them.

He left and headed home. He was going into the bar to work tonight. The bar was closed on Mondays, but his manager, D'Asia, and he usually came in for an hour once a month to plan the month.

"Nice crowd," he jokingly told D'Asia.

The woman smiled and said, "You're hilarious. What is on the agenda for the month?"

The work duo discussed plans for the week. He reminded her that the bar had an event next month and they had to send out marketing.

His bar made him about $150,000 a year, but after taxes and payroll, he took home about $50,000. That's all he needed in their city. That amount also was funds he used to assist Erika if needed.

After planning with D'Asia, Ron headed home. He wasn't going to see his grandson and daughter-in-law tonight, but he was looking forward to seeing them for the rest of the week.

Since Erika's nursing classes were in the morning, they decided two to three days out of the week, R3 would live with him. The other nights, she'd get the baby after she got off work around 6. He liked this setup because he received quality time with the baby, and Erika was able to rest.

He wasn't sure how she was going to keep her sanity while doing classes and working, but he was there for her.

The next morning Ron went to go pick up R3 from Erika's house. He assisted her with getting the baby ready. As she headed to class, he took the baby to the daycare.

When he signed in, Vanessa was helping to get the children in the classrooms and aiding the teachers.

"Great day to you, Mr. Ron," she greeted the 50-year-old man. "You too, Ron the Third." The young one walked to her and smiled.

"Same to you, dear," Ron said.

"I heard that you have a bar here in town," she said.

"It's true. You should come out sometime. It's one of the safest bars in town."

"I'll do that. I'll bring my best friend," she said.

"I look forward to seeing the both of you," he said. "Take care of my boy. I'll see you later."

"Likewise," she said, watching him leave.

She didn't know if he could tell, but she found him very attractive. She'd heard her coworkers say he was 50, but he didn't look to be out of his 30s. She herself was 24 but looked 20.

She knew black don't crack, but good grief, the man was a looker.

His salt and pepper afro always looked neat. He had pearly white teeth, and he seemed to be pretty fit. She also liked that she had to look up to look into his eyes.

Vanessa cleared her thoughts as she walked the young child to Tracy's class.

* * *

Tuesday turned into Wednesday. Wednesday turned into Thursday. Ron was off from the bar and took R3 to the daycare.

Tracy and Vanessa talked to him while he dropped the baby off.

"I'm not used to seeing a man working at a daycare. Why do you have a job at a daycare?" Ron asked.

"I've been babysitting since I was 15. I now get paid well enough for it."

"Do you enjoy it?"

"I love it," Tracy said. "Especially when I get kids with a great personality like Ron the Third."

The grandfather understood that statement. Ron has noticed that R3 was developing a personality, and it was nice to see it grow.

"What about you?" Ron asked Vanessa.

"I temporarily had custody of my niece when she was six months," Vanessa said. "I couldn't afford to pay for childcare. I paid a reduced fee at the daycare I worked at to have my niece there. I already had some childcare experience, so I was thankful it worked out. I can't let go of the childcare career yet, but I have other dreams and desires."

Ron was enthused.

This young lady was interesting.

* * *

It was Friday! Ron and Erika decided they would pick up Ron the Third together.

The young child was ecstatic to see both of them.

Vanessa came over and greeted both of them. She updated them on happenings at the daycare.

"You look great today," Vanessa told Erika. "What products are you using?"

The two ladies conversed as Ron chimed in occasionally.

"I'm telling you. You are a great conversation starter," Erika told her.

"Communication is my strong suit," Vanessa stated.

Vanessa switched her attention to Ron.

"What fountain of youth are you drinking from? I need to know."

Erika raised her eyebrow at the young lady as Ron responded.

"Erika and my grandbaby keep me young," he chirped.

"All that running after a one-year-old is working for you," Vanessa said.

"That's right, Pop," Erika said. "We need you here for a long time."

"See what you started?" Ron chuckled to Vanessa. "Health is wealth. Remember that."

Erika and Ron said bye to the girl.

Once the small family of three settled in the car, Erika blurted out, "Major flirt alert!"

"Me?" he inquired.

"No. The teacher. Pop, she wants you."

"She was just being nice."

"Are you sure?"

"You said it yourself," Ron said. "She's a conversation starter."

"Pop. She complimented you twice. Pay attention next week."

Ron looked at Erika. "That young girl not thinking about me," he said.

Erika stared back and said, "Pay attention."

* * *

Ron's weekend was packed. He didn't get a chance to visit Erika and R3. The only reason why he saw the young fella on Sunday was that Erika brought him over that night. She planned to pick him up Tuesday night from Ron's.

Ron and the baby watched *The Incredibles* that night before bed.

The next morning, he took Ron the Third to daycare. The daycare director and Vanessa talked to him. It was refreshing to see people other than his employees, Erika, and R3.

Tuesday morning when he arrived at the daycare. Vanessa wasn't there. He couldn't test Erika's theory. While he was heading out, he saw a car pull up. He heard a familiar song on the radio. It was "Always and Forever" by Heatwave.

He was shocked to see Vanessa get out of the car, quickly grabbing her items.

Ron walked over to her and asked, "Do you need help?"

She was originally going to say no, but once she saw that it was Ron, she said yes.

As he grabbed her things and helped walk her into the daycare, he asked, "How does a young lady like you know this song?"

The young woman grinned big and said, "I was raised around older folks. They always listened to songs like this. I fell in love with golden oldies like this one."

"At my bar we have 'Way Back Wednesdays' where

we play music from the 1960s to the 1980s. I think you should come out one night."

Vanessa was worried he might see her blushing.

"I'll do my best to come through," she told him when they made it inside. "Thank you, Mr. Ron."

"My pleasure, sweetheart," he said before exiting.

The next few days of the work week were a blur. He gave 110 percent to cater to Erika and R3, but it was Friday before he knew it. Fridays and Saturdays were his busiest nights. He usually helped his three employees out the most on those days.

It was 8 p.m., and things were starting to slow down for him and his staff. He knew another wave would start around 10 p.m. He was wiping down the bar when a voice chirped, "You keep a crowd here."

Ron was about to respond, but he looked in the person's direction.

"Well hello, sweetheart," he said when he recognized it was Vanessa.

"How are ya?" she asked him.

She batted her long lashes and looked at him.

The man was freshly groomed. That salt and pepper curly fro on his head still fit him.

"My customers keep me busy, and I love it," he said. "I'm glad you came out."

Ron waved to the friend she's brought with her.

He didn't want to look too hard, but he admired Vanessa's beauty. When she was at work, she kept it simple. She wore afro puffs or her hair in a tight afro. Her hair was in a coif today.

Those thick eyelashes did something for her face, and her lips looked like a Honeycrisp apple. He wanted to take a bite.

She was about to respond, and he was interested in listening, but D'Asia came to check in on him.

He apologized to her and went to help D'Asia settle a few things.

Ron came back to Vanessa and asked, "What can I do for you?"

She really wanted to tell him to fuck her brains out, but she refrained.

"We would like to order drinks," she said.

"ID please," he asked.

He ensured everything was accurate and was thankful to learn the young lady and her friend were 24.

Ron went to work on the drinks, and when he came back, he inquired, "What brought you two out?"

"Well, I'm always around babbling babies and

running toddlers. I figured tonight I would dress up and spend time with my bestie and visit your bar."

She was dressed indeed. Her green cutout shirt had her ample breasts on display. He wasn't sure what type of bottoms she was wearing, but he felt like they probably accentuated her figure.

Vanessa introduced him to her friend, and he told the ladies he had to go back to handling business.

As soon as he was gone, her friend said, "Are you sure that man is someone's grandfather? He is fine as hell."

"Girl!" Vanessa said. "I told you that man was a fine specimen. His grandson is a one-year-old at the daycare. He's single. I googled him a bit, and he's just a regular citizen in the city. He's had to bury a wife and a son. But he seems so positive. And he's always there for that baby and his daughter-in-law."

"You think he's crushing on you?" the friend asked.

"Probably not. He's probably too busy to think about me. But he's a great listener. He doesn't push me away when we talk at the daycare."

"That's saying a lot because you're a chatterbox."

The two busted out laughing, and Vanessa playfully pushed her friend.

The two stayed for another hour enjoying the liveliness of the bar. Ron checked in on them occasionally.

He was nervous about how many drinks they were throwing back.

But they assured him they had a ride home. When someone arrived, he was relieved to see Tracy.

"Tracy's my neighbor," Vanessa told Ron.

"Look at me babysitting on the weekends," Tracy joked with Ron.

"Please get them home safely."

He gave the girls a tray of fries and chicken wraps to sober up.

When the ladies left, he did take a peek at Vanessa one final time. She was charming. He knew it was probably wrong, but he looked at her backside. Her round derriere fit perfectly in a pair of green bell bottoms.

He had to question himself.

Was he attracted to Vanessa?

The weekend was over, and it was Monday morning. Ron didn't want to take R3 to daycare. The two spent a day in the city. They went to a locally owned toy store, grabbed lunch, and had fun. That night, Erika called and checked in on the boys via video call.

She was glad they'd had the opportunity to spend time together.

"So I think you're on to something," Ron said to Erika through the phone. "The teacher from the daycare came to the bar the other night," he said.

"I told you she wasn't crazy young," Erika said.

"Based on her ID, she is 24. We held a decent conversation, but I think she was being polite."

"Pop. I know you haven't dated anybody in years. If my hunch is correct, she likes you."

"But I don't like how it looks," he said. "You and my son are only four years older than her. I've never dated anyone that much younger than me."

"Just be open-minded," she said. "You don't have to fuck her or anything."

"Erika!" he said in disbelief. "Don't talk like that."

"Sorry, Pop. I just think you need a companion. Even if it's not long-term, Vanessa is engaging, and you need that. I don't want you to just see me and the baby all the time. Or just see your employees all the time."

"I know, baby girl," he said.

The family finished their video call.

The days rolled by, and it was Wednesday night.

Ron had a decent crowd at his establishment. He and D'Asia were running the business effortlessly as the golden oldies played music for "Way Back Wednesday."

He was taking the trash out the back when he saw Vanessa exiting a car and walking into the building. Maybe it wasn't her, but he wished it was. He went back inside to wash his hands and realized it was her.

Vanessa's orange two-piece top and skirt set fit her complexion beautifully. Her curls were on display tonight.

"What are you doing here?" Ron asked with a smile.

"I enjoyed myself last time. Plus the owner is very cute."

Ron played it cool and said, "Well, he does clean up nice. Thank you for coming. I hope you enjoy Way Back Wednesday. You look great, by the way."

"So do you," she said, admiring his fit.

It was a basic outfit, but he worked it well. It was a purple button-down short-sleeve shirt. He was probably wearing slacks.

His fro looked thicker than ever. His eyes and lips were like a finishing touch on him. His thick eyelashes played up his look. His lips looked supple.

"I know I will," she said, taking a seat.

They talked for a few minutes and enjoyed their time. He handled business for the bar as needed.

D'Asia came over and saw them having a good time.

"Hey boss," she said. "I have it over here. Go enjoy yourself."

"Thanks, D," he said to his employee.

"I got you," she said. D'Asia manned down the bar.

"Let me give you a tour of the place," Ron told Vanessa. "You haven't seen everything in the bar. We have about 1,800 square feet in the establishment. We do have some outside seats."

Ron walked her outside. There were about four tables with umbrellas on them and minimal decorations. He showed her the small selfie-station at about three tables. He said it was popular when Gen Z-ers and millennials come through.

Then he walked Vanessa to the bathrooms.

"If you notice, I have popular magazine covers on the walls in the bathroom."

"I see you're a boxing fan," she said, admiring the magazine covers in the bathroom.

"You nailed it on the head. I am."

Their final stop looked like a small locker room with a bathroom, microwave, and roundtable.

"This is our breakroom," he said. "When any of my employees are going through a hard time, I rearrange in here for them to put a mattress down and sleep."

"That's a beautiful thing," she said.

"I eventually want to get a contract with landlords in the area for my employees to live."

She was already attracted to him, but hearing his ideas made him more attractive.

"Your establishment is amazing," she told him.

"Thank you," he said.

"But Ron. I didn't just come to the bar for fun. I came here to tell you that I'm crushing on you."

"Me?" he asked.

"Yes you," she said, stepping closer to him. "At first, my crush was based on your looks. But the more I learn about you, the more I get attracted to you."

"I'm attracted to you too," he said. "But I'm not great with the dating game. Our age difference is not something I'm comfortable with."

"Now you know age ain't nothing but a number," she said.

"To me it's more than a number," he told her.

She held on to his arms and looked in his eyes.

"Who cares?" The vibes are here," she said. "There's already an attraction."

Ron couldn't deny the attraction. He also couldn't deny that it felt good having her on his body. He couldn't remember the last time he'd had a woman in his arms.

Could she tell how fast his heart was beating?

He looked down at her, and she puckered up her lips. Ron knew that was an invitation for a kiss. He leaned down and kissed her.

She realized not only were his lips soft, but they tasted minty.

Ron loved how her lips felt on his—nice and warm.

Vanessa didn't want the kiss to stop. But Ron pulled back.

"Do you need a drink or something?" he asked.

"Water please," she said.

"I'll get us a water," he said. "Stay here."

She smiled and obliged.

Ron was playing it off cool, but his insides were buzzing. He hoped this water would cool him down.

When he walked to the bar, he noticed the crowd was thinning out. He told D'Asia she could head out.

"I'll clean up tonight," he said. "Gather your things."

While she gathered her things, he went to check on Vanessa and passed her the water.

He walked D'Asia to her car and went back to Vanessa. He locked all the doors.

When he came back, Vanessa was in her bra and panties.

"I'm sorry about that. I just had to lock things up.

But I'm focused on you," he said. "You are so damn fine," he told her.

"Thank you, Ron," she said. "You would be as fine as me if you got out of those clothes and fucked me."

"Fuck you?" he said, biting his bottom lip. "Vanessa. I'm trying to be a gentleman, and you're making it hard for me."

"The only thing that needs to be hard is what is between your legs," she said to him.

"So we're doing this right now? Right here?"

"Right motherfucking here," she said before kissing his lips.

Sweet popping noises from their kissing filled the air. His hands couldn't help but travel from her upper back to her round ass. She squealed when he squeezed her derriere.

He liked that shit. So he did it again.

Ron was tired of being a gentleman.

The man quickly unbuttoned his shirt and started French kissing the beautiful woman. She moaned in between kisses and helped him take the shirt off. They threw it on the table.

In his eyes, it was sexy as hell to watch her furiously unbuckle his slacks and pull them down. He took his shoes off and stepped out of the pants.

He placed the pants on one of the chairs in the breakroom and pulled her into his lap. They were hungry for each other. Their grips were tight on each other. The kissing was more intense. They were leaving marks on each other's bodies. Their entire moment was pure euphoria for the both of them. They were in their own world, and Ron didn't mind.

Right now, nothing else mattered but to pleasure themselves.

Vanessa was grinding on the bulge in his underwear. His penis was fighting him. He was ready to release his flesh and put it in her.

Ron raked his fingers in between her curls. One hand slightly choked her as he kissed her.

"Yes," she breathed out. "Just like this. I want you in me."

That sentence was the passcode for him to open up.

He stretched his shirt across the table and placed her on top of it. She leaned back on her elbows. He pulled her as close to the edge as he could. He lowered his body to get eye to eye with her honeypot. He opened her legs wider and started feasting on her sensitive flesh.

Her body trembled from his lips kissing on her thighs. His lips came into contact with her honeypot lips, and she let out a whimper.

"My goodness," she said as his wet mouth muscle slid and glided in many ways to pleasure her. Her nipples were getting hard, and she was tingling all over. She played with her breasts as he continued to devour her. She rocked herself on his tongue before he pulled out.

The man delved two fingers in her as he sucked on her clit.

Vanessa's sensual tones got louder, and Ron continued to pleasure her. Ron was always a giver, and hearing her respond to him was keeping his penis hard as a rock.

His neck was starting to hurt. He figured that was his age catching up to him.

He stood up and stroked himself. Vanessa thought he looked so sexy with his hefty penis in his hand.

She watched as he came to her face with a final kiss.

She looked down at him as his tip grazed the folds of her honeypot several times before he finally slid in.

"Shit," they said in unison.

Ron felt like he was about to nut. He pulled out.

"What's wrong?" she asked.

"I think I have to pace myself," he said. "I'm sorry. I won't last long."

"I don't care if you're a minute man," she said.

All she wanted was him inside of her.

"Thank God," he said placing himself back in her.

Vanessa couldn't tell if it was her imagination or

what, but he fit her so perfectly. Her honeypot was so full of him.

"Fuck. You're gripping me," he said as he moved slowly inside of her.

She locked eyes with him, and he didn't want to let her face out of his sight.

Ron's eyes were glued to hers as she gripped his manhood. The room was softly spinning as he had the table rocking, and her honeypot was gushing loudly.

He grunted as he pulled out, stroked himself, and nutted on her stomach.

The liquid was hot on her skin, but all she could say was, "Put it back in."

She realized he wasn't joking. He really did last only a minute.

He listened to the beauty beneath him and went back in.

Ron felt like he was swimming in a hot spring that was made for him. He felt like he was going to get lost in her waters if he went too deep. She was like a siren calling him to be with her in this moment. He was going to glide into her waters until she hit ecstasy.

He pulled her face to his chest and held on to her as he continued to submerge himself in her.

"Please don't stop," she pleaded. She was not about to hit her climax, but it felt so good to her.

He kissed her and continued to give her the business.

Vanessa was glad he was lasting this time. They were both starting to sweat, and their breathing was haggard.

Ron walked them back to the chair. He let her ride.

He was so glad he did.

She rocked and rolled on his dick like she was at a rodeo. Their room was filled with their bodies slapping and clapping for each other.

"I'm about to come," she told him.

"Good," he said. "Get that shit."

"Look me in my eyes," she commanded him.

The two looked at each other as he talked her into getting to her peak. Vanessa held on to the back of the chair as they worked together to get her there.

"Oh my God!" she cried out as her release hit her body.

Ron grabbed her ass cheeks and continued to bounce her up and down as she came undone on him.

The woman was now whimpering his name as she held on for life.

He could feel her honeypot clenching on him, and he loved the filling.

When she came back to her senses, he came in her honeypot.

"Fuck!" he whimpered as he kissed her. He could still feel himself spilling in her.

She didn't mind, though. She wanted this intimacy with him.

He wrapped her arms around his neck and said, "I have to pull out."

"No," she pleaded. She liked the feeling of having him inside of her.

He placed subtle kisses on her lips.

Her honeypot was wrapped around him tightly, and he didn't want to let go, but he couldn't fuck her all night.

They both had somewhere important to be the next morning—the daycare.

He carefully pulled out and placed her in the chair.

"Are you okay?" he asked her.

"I'd be even better if you fucked me again."

He was glad she'd enjoyed their time together but said, "If I had more time, I would. But you know I have to help get the baby to the daycare in the morning."

He grabbed the pieces of her suit and helped her put them on.

She was glad he did because she couldn't concentrate. She was still in the moment.

"At least let me help you straighten up the place," she said, gathering her composure and trying to stand.

Ron caught her and said, "I gave it to you so good you can't walk straight?"

"I mean you nutted so fast the first time. It happened in a blink. But that second time was something way more eventful."

Ron understood where she was coming from. His wife had died eight years ago, but he'd had sex for the first time a year ago. So his dick wasn't used to getting pussy.

She helped him clean the business. He walked her to her car and kissed her passionately.

He didn't want the night to end, but he had to stay focused.

"I'll see you in the morning?" he inquired.

"You'll see me then," she said.

The man smiled as he walked to his car. He wasn't sure if that was a one-time thing or not, but he wanted more of Vanessa.

The next morning Ron helped get R3 ready for the daycare. He couldn't stop thinking about Vanessa. He couldn't stop thinking about what they'd done the night before either.

Ron wanted to treat the day like a regular day, but he was excited to see Vanessa.

She looked good this morning. Her hair was in afro puffs, and she was in a casual pink dress. It was modest for work, but he could still see her shape.

She greeted him and R3 like nothing had transpired the night before. She treated them like she normally did.

Ron couldn't tell if he was worried about it or not.

After making sure R3 was okay, Ron walked to his car.

Vanessa followed him outside.

"Hey, Ron. I wanted to know if you wanted to go on a date sometime next week?" she said.

"A date? I would like that." He smiled.

He passed her his business card and said, "Call or text me?"

Vanessa hugged him and said, "Say less."

Ron entered his car and thought about everything that had transpired in the last eight hours.

For the first time in a long time, he felt like his future would be bright.

Thank you!

So, my queens, how did you enjoy Black Erotica?

I'd love some feedback!

It would mean the world to me if you would take a moment to review this book on Amazon or Audible. It'll just take you a few seconds, and it would really help this project find an audience.

Thank you so much. We're already working on a sequel.

XOXO,

Jade.

www.ingramcontent.com/pod-product-compliance
Lightning Source LLC
Chambersburg PA
CBHW071932190726
48293CB00004B/1245